The Sigil Five

AND

Dragos Primeri Stories

Natalie Wright

Illustrations by

Félix Farley

Tucson

Published by Menaris Books, Tucson, Arizona.

NatalieWright@NatalieWrightAuthor.com.

Identifiers: LCCN 2025923089 (print)
ISBN 9798992152142

CONTENTS

For The Dragos Primeri
Street Team & Fans ♥

The Sigil Five

Chapter One

With a cup of Bardivian gold in one hand and a dagger in the other, Octavia inched toward the man she'd kill today. Matron Fortunata would soon bestow the coveted Domanulos sigil ring on her cousin Brádach, sealing his ascension to Māja Babesta's inner circle.

And Octavia intended to prevent it.

Having never killed before, Octavia needed to fortify her courage. She sipped the wine and reminded herself what a banch-nagging pustule Brádach was. Brádach's father, Batiste, sat at his side, and there mere sight of her uncle made her lip curl in disgust. He—Batiste—was the true enemy of Octavia and the entire house. But the Domanulos ring already bound to Batiste made him nearly impossible to eliminate. *To end Batiste's line, I must snip his branch and must do it tonight, before Brádach receives the protection of the sigil ring.*

Octavia glanced behind, and her eyes landed on her bodyguard, Rignar[1]. He stood at the edge of the crowd, dutifully watching for threats against her. Fortunately for Octavia, he didn't know of her plan, or he'd have tried to stop her.

She gripped the dagger in her sweaty palm and took a deep, calming breath. Octavia focused on Brádach and edged closer.

Cousin Junia's voice rang out. "There you are. I've searched everywhere for you." Her beaded hair clacked as she walked. Junia swept her arms wide, inviting a hug, and wine sloshed from her cup as she staggered toward Octavia.

Already tippled, Octavia thought.

Octavia slipped the dagger into the sleeve pocket of her long coat and flashed Junia a false smile.

"Dearest cousin," Octavia said. Standing a full head taller than diminutive Junia, Octavia stooped to return her cousin's embrace and

---

[1] Rignar Nyanja di Shills, aka "Aldewin di Partha".

kisses. Junia smelled of thrumian spice, jessamine blossoms and wine.

Junia grabbed Octavia's cup and downed the remaining wine in one gulp. She wiped wine from her lips and smiled. "You're drinking the good stuff." She raised an eyebrow and gave Octavia a derisive laugh. "So you're celebrating then? I hardly thought you'd be happy about Brádach's ascension."

Octavia snatched her cup back, but didn't answer. She returned her attention to the dais where Brádach sat, awaiting the Domanulos ceremony. Fortunata, Matron of Māja Babesta, would place the house sigil ring on his finger, and everyone would politely applaud, though most members of Māja Babesta disliked Brádach nearly as much as they detested his father.

Junia hooked an arm in Octavia's. She followed her cousin's gaze, then patted the hard steel she felt in Octavia's sleeve. Junia stomped on Octavia's toe. "Don't do anything stupid."

Octavia raised the cup to her lips, and too-late realized Junia had drained it. "I'm doing what needs done to secure the future of our house." She placed the empty cup on a passing server's tray and moved toward the dais, but Junia held her back.

"Look at me," Junia said. "Even if you kill him, you'll never ascend to the Cordomis."

"Eleventh in line, I wasn't going to anyway. But at least Brádach won't. Rumor has it, he's as odious as his father, and for the same reason," Octavia said.

"Those rumors are true." Junia's mirth was gone, and her jaw twitched.

"For the sake of the house, especially its youth, you understand why I must do this," Octavia said. "And now, before the Domanulos goes on his slimy finger. Once it binds to him, the sigil will make it nearly impossible to steal, and it will protect his disgusting ass."

"All true," Junia said.

"Matron Fortunata favors house members who triumph at the game," Octavia said.

"Also correct."

Octavia sighed and patted the blade hidden in her sleeve. "Then why should I not plunge this steel into his wormy fucking gut?"

"For the love of Jantu's balls, Tavi, you need a triumph, not a Shills-style half rate hit. You could hire your man Rignar to do that."

Rig was near enough to pounce, yet distant enough not to overhear their whispers. His expression was stoic detachment, his gaze expertly shifting across the room, watching for danger. Yet Octavia knew he was anything but detached or stoic about defending her. *What would Father say if he knew I'd taken Rig as my lover?*

Returning her focus to Junia, Octavia said, "Hiring a Vandu assassin takes no finesse."

Junia grabbed fresh wine cups and inclined her head toward the balcony patio. Tavi followed, and she felt Rignar sweep through the crowd behind her, following like an ever-present shadow.

Once clear of the crowd, Junia handed Tavi a goblet and whispered. "Matron Fortunata values guile. Subtlety. Artfulness. And she adores the long game."

"You're not a member of the Cordomis. How do you know what grandmother adores?"

"I have my ways," Junia said. Mischief twinkled in her eyes. "Look, if you kill Brádach in such a crass way, Fortunata will shun you. You must play a sophisticated game. Take risks. Do this, Tavi, and grandmother will reward you."

Octavia thought Junia would talk her out of even entering the bloodsport of Māja politics and intrigues. Tavi was the eighth of Mistress Fortunata's grandchildren, and eleventh in the line of succession. Her role was to support those above her, not leapfrog over them. Since Junia was ahead of her in the leadership queue, Tavi had assumed it served Junia's interests to keep Tavi right where she was.

Rig melted into the shadows by the door. Tavi didn't understand how someone so tall could vanish so thoroughly. She caught his eye, and he gave her a single nod, then returned to his stoic surveillance.

Tavi sipped the vinegary red and puckered. Batiste, the cheap bastard, was serving wine only a step above vinegar. "What do you suggest, dear cousin?" Tavi asked.

"To gain Fortunata's attention—in a good way—you must pull off an audacious plan. Something none have yet achieved," Junia said.

"Sounds like you have something in mind," Tavi said.

Junia chuckled. "What if we solve two problems at once?"

"Go on."

"Cousin Brádach is bothersome, to be sure, but his father is an absolute menace. Since he is first in the line of succession…"

Tavi nearly choked on her wine. "Are you suggesting… You can't possibly propose—"

"Batiste," Junia said.

Tavi shook her head. "He already wears the Domanulos. No, it's impossible."

"Not if you use your available assets."

"Maybe you're forgetting. The ring is theft proof. Māja Artifexa makes sure of that when they craft the rings," Tavi said.

Junia groaned and thumped Tavi's head. Rig sprung and bolted to Tavi's side, ready to protect her from her cousin's assault.

"My cousin merely jests," Tavi said.

He frowned and kept his hand on the hilt of his Vandu blade. Tavi smiled and waved him off. Apparently satisfied that Junia wasn't a threat, he gave Tavi a nod and returned to his spot by the door.

Junia continued. "Think, Tavi. Do you know someone impervious to the Domanulos' poison?" Her gaze flitted to Rignar. "Perhaps someone who is already under your command?"

As the realization dawned, Tavi's heart thundered. Her eyes, too, landed on Rig.

"To become a member of the Cordomis, you must do two things above all else. First, please Fortunata."

"And you think she'd reward someone who killed her son?" Tavi asked.

"People whisper that Matron Fortunata is quite unhappy with Batiste." Junia pressed even closer and lowered her voice further. "A trusted source heard Fortunata say, 'Even a venerable seed can grow a twisted plant warped by disease,' and 'Sometimes you must pluck the pestilence out and begin again.'"

Tavi laughed. "Was she talking about Batiste or her garden?"

Junia did not laugh. "Trust me on this. Grandmother Fortunata was *definitely* referring to Batiste. Anyway, to rise in Māja Babesta you must win Fortunata's favor and be audacious. Take the Domanulos off that pervert's dead hand and place it on yours. Steal his Domanulos and you gain his estate. Do this, and Mistress Fortunata will respect you, not disgrace you."

Tavi's heart raced with the excitement of possibility. If she succeeded with Junia's plan, she'd not only prove her worth, she'd take all that Batiste has: His seat on the Cordomis, his wealth, his housing compound, his dominion over his vassals, and even command of his children.

Her gaze again found Brádach. Not one to hold back on lording his lofty station over everyone, Tavi generally avoided Brádach's company. *Ironic that I could become* his *master.* Tavi's commitment to the idea Junia planted grew with each passing second.

As much as Junia's proposal excited Octavia, she had doubts. Junia and she shared closeness, yet no one within Māja Babesta offered help without expecting a return.

"Your idea intrigues me." Tavi narrowed her eyes at Junia. "But what do you gain, dear cousin?"

"Besides seeing that Batiste never touches another girl or boy again?" Her expression looked like she'd tasted something sour. "While that would suffice, in truth, your success will move my mother up to first in line. And the rats whisper Fortunata would be most pleased for my mother, Eligia, to succeed her rather than Batiste."

"Then why don't you do it? Or your brother Gavino? He's wily," Tavi said.

Junia nodded toward Rig. "We don't have a Vandu at our command."

Tavi followed Junia's gaze. He must have sensed her stare, because he gave her a small smile.

Rig was a newly minted Vandu assassin, and the youngest to have ever survived the arduous trials. Fen Menir wouldn't allow him to remain a bodyguard for the eleventh heir to Fortunata's legacy. Soon, they'd reassign him, and she'd lose not only her highly skilled guard, but her lover and friend. *Perhaps my only true friend.*

Junia's plan to steal Batiste's sigil ring presented many concerns and challenges. The assassination of Batiste wouldn't be Fen Menir sanctioned. If Rig didn't succeed, Tavi couldn't protect him from Fen Menir. *Am I asking too much of him?*

But if they succeeded, Tavi would hold wealth second only to Fortunata and leapfrog to second in line to succeed her. She'd be able to buy Rig's remaining indenture. *And set him free.*

'Oft times, sacrifice is required to secure one's station,' Fortunata often said.

Tavi hoped that whatever sacrifice the gods demanded wasn't too high a price to pay.

CHAPTER TWO

In the long history of the Mājas, nobody had successfully purloined a Domanulos. Māja Artifexa, the house of crafts, arts, and magic, ensured that each ring worn by a Mājas Cordomis—or "Heart of the House" inner circle—contained a sigil imbued with magical properties. Its key feature: Impervious to theft.

Achieving such a feat…

Tavi tossed her long coat onto a bench and flung off her shoes. She nearly toppled and grabbed the bedpost to keep from falling. *Too much wine.* She hiccupped and tried to undo the clasp on her gold-beaded choker, but her fingers weren't working properly.

"Allow me." His voice was a low breath on her neck. His deft fingers on her skin sent waves of heat through her. Rig's nimble fingers undid the clasp, and he caught the necklace before it fell, his fingers sweeping like a breeze over her chest.

Tavi hadn't heard him enter her suite. He moved with the shadows and had arrived through her hidden passage. *He's perfect for the Domanulos heist.*

She pressed against him in all the right places. Octavia offered her lips. "You will stay the night, yes?"

Rig wound a firm arm around her waist, kissed her deeply, and said, "No."

His defiance nearly extinguished the building fire. "No?" She tittered. "You mistake me. That was a command, not a question."

He sighed. "Octavia, dearest mistress of mine, you are quite intoxicated, and therefore not in possession of your ability to consent or withhold. Therefore, I'm within my right, as your vassal, to deny your request."

Tavi rolled her eyes and made a talking motion with her hands. "Blah, blah. Boring legal mumbling. Blah. Your Fen Menir masters filled your head with too much drudgery during your

Vandu trials. You're becoming a bore, Rig." She feigned a pout.

Reaching back to undo the buttons of her thin silk shift, she struggled and again, nearly fell. Rig caught her before she collapsed.

"Should I call for your dressing assistant?" he asked.

Tavi pressed into him again. "She smells of cabbage." Tavi's nose wrinkled. "And her fingers are icy."

He chuckled. "That sounds unpleasant."

Tavi turned her face up to him. "You do it."

Rig groaned like she'd asked him to roast his own balls on a grill. He muttered under his breath. "You test me more than the Vandu trials and may be the death of me someday." He complained but unfastened the buttons.

Tavi turned and allowed the shift to fall. She wore no underclothes. His gaze languid, he didn't allow his eyes to rove over her body. Instead, Rig maintained eye contact.

On tiptoes, her pert breasts pressed to him, Tavi swirled her tongue in his ear. "You enjoy torture, don't you sweet Rignar?" One hand undid the laces of his shirt, while the other cupped his manhood. He could deny that he loved her, and even pretend he didn't intend to bed her, but his hardness proved he was anything but neutral about Tavi.

She planted feathery kisses on his now-bared chest. Her voice low and sultry, she said, "Because you're assigned to me, I hold your contract. Your very life is in my hands." Tavi gave his nethers a squeeze to punctuate her point.

He neither spoke nor embraced her.

"By writ, you must do as I command." She nibbled his ear and undid his pants laces. "And what if I command you to kill Batiste?"

He scoffed. "Batiste? If rumors about him are true—"

"They are." She scowled.

"Then he deserves a slow torturous death, not the quick, virtually painless death from a kiss of the Night Sister's Vandu blade."

Tavi continued kissing his chest and neck though Rig didn't return her affections. "True. Batiste deserves suffering. But killing Batiste opens a path to many things." Frustrated by his lack of reciprocation of her affections, Tavi sighed. "I could command you to kill him, but I prefer if you agree."

Rig remained stoic. "I must follow your command in most things, that is true. You are mistaken on one point though, Mistress. Killing a member of the Cordomis must be sanctioned by Fen Menir."

"Rules." She tsked. "Rules are meant to be broken." Tavi kissed him again. "What if you could be free of Fen Menir's shackles?"

He didn't answer, but also didn't bat her hands away.

Her voice became earnest. "This will alter our destinies, Rig. What do you say?"

"I'm listening."

She kissed him again, and this time he returned her affection.

The possibility of a future with Rig—as an equal rather than a servant—sobered Tavi. She hugged him and caught his eye. "One death, Rig. That is all I ask. A strategic kill, and I hold the power of that loathsome prig's sigil. One kill, dearest, and I will possess the ability to purchase your remaining indenture. Kill Batiste, and you are free of Fen Menir."

Her lips found his, and this time he wound his arms around her. His tongue darted into her mouth, and his hands were everywhere all at once.

Tavi's heart hammered. Her voice was breathless. "Help me with this, my assassin, and you will be free."

Rig met her gaze. "Even if you cut Fen Menir's strings, I'll still be ensnared by you, Tavi."

In one swift move, Rig lifted her onto the bed. He gently parted her thighs and kissed her deeply there, sealing their bargain with Tavi's favorite kind of kiss.

Chapter Three

Rig departed before Tavi rose from her slumber. She wasn't proud of using her feminine guile to lure him into her scheme, but in hindsight, throwing herself at him hadn't secured his assent. No, she dangled the right carrot by promising Rig his deepest desire.

Freedom.

Tavi knew he despised his indentured status. Not enslaved exactly, but not totally free, either. He could roam the city at will, even leave Partha to adventure for a time. But ultimately, Fen Menir held his leash, able to call upon him at any time to perform services under a contract. If he did not obey…

He is a wild stallion, never suited to being trapped into captivity.

To pull off the Domanulos heist, she'd need more than one freshly minted Vandu assassin. She needed a tactical plan and the personnel to pull it off. And she knew where to begin.

Her cousin Junia's younger brother, Gavino, spent too much time drinking and losing money, but he'd been great friends with Brádach in their youth. He knew Batiste's compound better than either she or Junia.

Tavi invited her cousins for luncheon to discuss the Domanulos heist. Servants arranged a spread of finger foods in Tavi's solar, where they would have the utmost privacy. Rig had swept all passageways for unwanted intruders and stood guard at the door.

She was reluctant to pull Gavino into the scheme. Tavi loved her cousin well, but one could never be certain of motivations and loyalties within the ever-shifting winds of Māja Babesta.

Even Junia's true intent remained a mystery. She'd said she had a vested interest in Tavi's success, but Junia could just as readily hope for her failure, which would disgrace Tavi's entire family. That could be enough to knock Tavi's father, Lorencio, from the Cordomis, thus opening space for Junia.

In private, Rig had pointed out his concerns about Junia's loyalty. "She profits as much from your half-success as from a perfect triumph," he'd said.

"How so?"

"If, using me, you eliminate Batiste from the board but fail to capture his signet's power, then Junia wins even more."

"How dare you suggest my dear cousin would use me that way? We have always been the closest of friends and holders of each other's secrets. She has never betrayed me," Tavi had said.

Rig gave her a roguish grin.

"What's so amusing? I'm truly furious with you."

"Did you know you get an adorable crinkle between your eyes when you're cross?"

Tavi smoothed the skin between her eyes with her thumb. "No, I didn't know that and now, thanks to you, I'll be forever self-conscious of it."

His earnest demeanor returned. "Look, Tavi, you're naïve at this game."

Tavi laughed. "And you, still shy of your eighteenth birthday, know more about Babesta machinations than I do? I've lived in this Māja my entire life, Rig. Do not forget who you speak to."

Questioning Junia's motivations had annoyed her, but impugning Tavi's skill at the game stoked her ire.

Rig's mirth gone, his face returned to the practiced stoic mask of his Vandu assassin persona. "And you, Mistress, should not forget who *you* speak to. I am Fen Menir, trained since my childhood to serve only Night's Sister. Before attaining my first blade at twelve, my ears and eyes served my true Mistress, Sicara. I've listened to plots and schemes of Mājas my whole life. And trust me, Babesta's schemes are relatively bloodless and straightforward compared to Wix. Mistress Idaya is…"

"What is she?"

He waved her off. "A story for another time, perhaps. About my misgivings, know that I want your plan to succeed." He'd taken her hand. "I'm on your side."

She believed he was.

Rig continued. "I've observed twisted machinations planned over decades and unfolded over years. I have faith that one day you will be among the best at the game. But if you trust Junia wholly… Well, members of Babesta should not trust their cousins, even ones who are friends."

He'd given her much to ponder, and also made her anxious. Though he'd intended to make her wary of Junia, Rig had also increased her anxiety about Rig.

Rignar had come into her employ a year ago. A young and green guard.

Tavi's father, Lorencio, hired Fen Menir bodyguards for his entire family. Not unusual for those with seats on the Cordomis.

Lorencio had been upset with Ser Mélantos, Master of Fen Menir house, for assigning such a young guard for Tavi. But Mélantos had assured Lorencio that Rig's skill exceeded many older members of Fen Menir. And once Tavi met Rignar, she'd lobbied with vigor for Rig to remain.

In the end, she doubted her entreaties had swayed her father. That Fen Menir tapped Rig to participate in the Vandu trials won her father over. Failure at the trials meant Rignar would be dead, and Fen Menir would have assigned a new guard for Tavi. But if Rig succeeded, Lorencio's compound would be the only one in Babesta with a Vandu assassin in its employ. A great boon, given that a Vandu was impervious to poisons and toxins and masterful with a blade.

It was less than ideal to bring two of her aunt Eligia's children into her scheme, but Tavi had no choice. Rig was right. Tavi had little experience with the game, while Gavino had served as tactician for one of his mother's plots, and Junia the gadfly always possessed deep knowledge of gossip and goings-on within the Māja.

Gavino swept into the solar, and they exchanged kisses and an embrace. He then complained about her chosen venue. "Really, Tavi? Your solar?" He tutted. "We're children no longer." Gavino proffered a pout. "You're asking me to practically camp in the Vats." His eyes roved the room. "Please tell me you at least have wine."

Tavi poured him a cup as Junia glided into the sun-drenched room. She snatched a cup from the sideboard and held it out for Tavi to pour. "Drink your wine, little brother, and stop haranguing my favorite cousin. Tavi has her reasons." Junia gave Tavi a wink.

Tavi gestured for Rig to close the doors and offered her guests a seat at the round table at the room's center.

Gavino, seeing that Tavi had dismissed all servants except for her bodyguard, quickly got the drift. He raised his goblet to Tavi. "Ah, I see. Our sweet young cuz has joined the great game. Then we shall toast to you, Tavi."

They clinked their cups, and Gavino sipped his wine. His eyes twinkled with mischief.

"Count me in," Gavino said.

Tavi laughed. "You don't even know what the game is yet? Once you hear, you might be less enthusiastic."

Junia popped spiced almonds into her mouth. "Or more enthusiastic." Her gaze landed on Gavino, her look intense.

As if a hidden meaning passed between them, Gavino refocused on Tavi, his expression now more earnest. He pulled his chair closer. "It's not like my sister to be so serious." He stroked his close-cropped beard. "Now, I *must* know."

Tavi drank deeply, sighed, and gave a furtive look back at the door. "Okay, first, remember that this was actually Junia's idea."

Gavino raised an eyebrow at his sister.

"Just ushering our sweet cuz into the game. Go on, Tavi. Tell him," Junia said.

"Well, in brief, we're going to purloin an object of great value. One not easily lifted," Tavi said.

"First foray into the game and you lead with audacious boldness? I like it!" Gavino filled a small plate with fruit and cheese. "Please continue. I'm all ears."

"We're going to steal Uncle Batiste's Domanulos," Tavi said.

Gavino choked on his wine. He wiped his mustache. "Jantu's balls, Tavi." Gavino cast a sideways glance at Junia. "Your idea, huh sis?" His tone accused.

Junia didn't wither under his gaze. "I want neither credit nor outcome's prize or fortune. All benefits to Tavi."

Gavino stroked his beard. "You both know my loathing for this particular Domanulos signet wearer. The vile pustule passing for human—well, if someone were to rub him out, I would cheer rather than shed a tear."

Both women raised their cups. The three clinked their goblets and silently drank to their uncle's speedy demise.

"But that bit about stealing his sigil's power." Gavino tsked. "Tricky business, that." He nodded toward Rig, who remained motionless yet alert at the door. "Even your Vandu man there…"

Tavi sighed. "Look, if it weren't difficult, someone would have done it before. If it were easy, it wouldn't be the sort of daring scheme to garner Fortunata's favor. In my position, my moves must be bold, or why make them at all?"

Gavino's expression softened. "Okay, Tavi. Tell me your plan for achieving the unachievable."

"Well, I have ideas, but that's why you're here, cousin. To help me plan this heist."

Gavino chuckled and raised his wine cup. "I spend more time drinking and gambling than organizing schemes."

"Maybe," Tavi said. "But you know Batiste's compound—and his weaknesses—better than most."

Gavino didn't disagree. He pondered, then asked, "What will distract Batiste?"

"Wine?" Junia said.

"No—well, yes, to a degree. We'll certainly use the dulling effects of the vine, but that's not the chief attraction," Gavino said.

"A mirror?" Tavi laughed. "To gaze upon his favorite view—himself."

The three chuckled, then Gavino said, "True. but no, not a mirror. Think my friends. What is

Batiste's ultimate weakness?" His expression turned dour. "The thing that makes us all despise him and his wrinkled little prick so much?"

"Of course," Junia said. She chortled. "Brilliant."

Tavi shook her head. "I've missed something. What are you talking about?"

"The distraction, dear cousin. Something irresistible to capture dear Uncle Batiste's rapt attention while we work the scheme."

Tavi blinked.

"A woman. A *young* woman," Gavino said.

"We can't just throw a young innocent into his lair," Tavi said. "But of course, you frequent places where one might get to know certain—people…"

Gavino tutted. "Now, don't judge, cuz." He glanced at Rig. "Not everyone has—access—to captive entertainment like *some* people do."

Tavi caught his meaning, and her neck flushed. Normally, she would have met the comment with a barbed insult. But she needed Gavino's help and his assets. *Part of learning the game. Not rising to the bait.*

She raised her cup to him. "Touché."

Gavino smiled and gave her a wink. "Yes, I know of the perfect distraction. A dear friend, Sabine."

"The famed ember dancer?" Junia asked.

"The very one," Gavino said.

"They're quite rare, aren't they?" Tavi asked.

"Exceptionally rare in Partha, but more are coming up from Qülla these days. Sabine's dance is—well, Batiste will be the envy of the Mājas if he received a gift of a private ember dance on his birthday," Gavino said.

Tavi's heart fluttered with excitement at the idea. Gavino was right. Her perverted uncle would never turn down the opportunity for a private ember dance.

"Well, now I know what we're getting our dear uncle for his birthday," Tavi said.

"Perfect," Junia said. Her eyes twinkled. "Okay, you have your hit man." She nodded at Rig. "And we have a plan for a distraction."

Rig came forward. "The ember dancer will distract Batiste, but you must distract two men that night," he said.

Gavino appraised Rig appreciatively and raised an eyebrow. "And he speaks, too."

Tavi kicked her cousin under the table. "Behave." She turned her attention to Rig. "Ah yes, Batiste's personal guard."

Rig nodded. "As you know, I am forbidden from unsanctioned assassinations of other members of Fen Menir, so I cannot simply kill his guard. You need a plan to divert Batiste's guard from his duties so I have access to Batiste to make the kill."

Rig rarely spoke, and she'd never heard him talk with such authority before. Tavi wished they were alone so she could show Rig just how much she enjoyed listening to him talk business.

"Batiste's personal guard is old Gerard. Not a Vandu, and he loves his wine cup nearly as much as Batiste does," Gavino said.

"Does he drink on the job?" Junia asked.

"He is known to," Gavino said. He winked at Junia. "And I'm sure you can persuade him to join you for some wine, dear sister."

"And a sleeping draught in his wine is even better," Rig said.

"You're not a member of Māja Babesta," Junia said. She sneered at Rig. "Each of us has a role to play, and yours is to be the brawn, not the brains."

Tavi had heard her cousin speak this way to servants, but had not expected Junia to regard

Rig, a Vandu assassin and her lover, as a mere servant. About to scold her cousin, Rig said, "I apologize, Mistress Junia. I did not mean to offend you, but only to offer assistance to my mistress."

Junia waved him off with a flick of her thin hand.

"Are you done?" Gavino directed his question to Junia and glared at her. "Rignar offered sound advice. Don't be so haughty."

Junia rolled her eyes and ignored Gavino. "Yes, I can handle Gerard as Tavi's vassal guard suggested. Now, let us proceed to the matter of gaining entry to Batiste's personal chambers within his compound. We need a lock expert."

"It should be easy enough for Rig to pick a lock on a door," Tavi said. "I've seen him do this before. You can do this, can't you, Rig?"

He began to answer, but before he could speak, Junia interrupted him.

"Batiste must know that many would like to see him removed from the board. The number of guards and sophisticated locks, not to mention magical wards… No simple lock-picking will suffice."

"Right you are, sister. Save for the actual transfer of the sigil's power, this is the most difficult tactical aspect of this heist," Gavino said.

Though Junia had tried to silence him, her attempts to diminish Rig hadn't cowed him. "I know someone perfect for this job," he said.

"You know someone skilled at gaining entry into Māja compounds?" Tavi asked.

"I know several, actually, but one owes me for—a favor, shall we say? Her name is Cleo."

"Cleo," Tavi repeated. Her eyes narrowed, and her jaw set. "I like it. Women should be involved in ending him."

"Dear uncle is despised by plenty of men, too," Gavino added, his voice grave. "I don't care about the lock master's gender. I just need to know she's got the required skills."

Junia turned her attention to Rignar. Her tone was derisive. "Shills locks are one thing. But Māja locks are quite another, Vandu boy."

"I'm well aware, Māja girl," Rig said. His tone brooked no argument. "I wouldn't have suggested Cleo if I didn't know she has the required aptitude for this job."

Hearing her Rignar fight back against her cousin's curt derisiveness made Tavi's nipples perky, and emboldened her. Tavi glared at Junia. "Don't forget yourself, cousin. Rig is a Vandu assassin, not a boy. Show respect."

Rig's hand had found its way to the hilt of his Vandu blade, and his jaw twitched. Ever since Fen Menir awarded him the Vandu blade, Tavi had noticed how quickly his hand found it whenever he felt remotely threatened. With his fingers on the hilt, Rig's demeanor changed from easygoing to threatening.

Junia visibly blanched and pressed back into her seat.

Tavi had never gotten the upper hand with anyone in her Māja before. The adrenaline rush proved intoxicating. *If this is power, I want more.*

"Cleo for lock duty, then," Tavi said. She raised her goblet. "To Cleo, our lock master."

The other two drank a toast with her, but their demeanor had shifted. Gavino's light mood vanished, and he squirmed uncomfortably in his seat.

Perhaps sensing their unease at his proximity, Rig bowed slightly and returned to his post.

"We've made much progress today," Gavino said at last. "Assuming we have no issues securing Sabine and Cleo, our team is set."

"What else can I do, cousin, to aid your efforts?" Junia asked. Her tone had returned to amiable.

"Your job is to ensure Batiste has a grand party for his birthday," Gavino said. "We need him stuffed with food and drunk on wine."

"And his guard will be more easily enticed to imbibe if the atmosphere is convivial," Tavi said.

"This I can do," Junia said.

"Perfect," Tavi said. "With me, Rignar, Sabine, Cleo, and Gavino, our team that night will be five strong." She thought for a moment, then raised her goblet one last time. "Our heist will be in the hands of the Sigil Five."

"To the Sigil Five," Gavino said.

"Yes, to the Sigil Five," Junia said. Her eyes narrowed at Tavi as she sipped her wine. "May the leader of the Five remember always those who supported her ascension."

Tavi gave her a nod and drained her cup. *And may I survive this without a knife in my back.*

CHAPTER FOUR

The aroma of sea air, dead fish, and piss wafted to Tavi as she and Rig wove their way through the throngs near the docks. Tavi had rarely left the rarefied air of Partha's walled portion, within which all the Māja compounds had been built, and she certainly had never visited the seedy dockside area known as the Shills.

Following Rig's advice, she'd forgone her usual silks and donned a simple linen shirt, breeches, and a wool cloak. Rig had scrounged the clothes from somewhere. They were clean, but the crude fabric made her itch. *Or maybe it's the lice on the heads around me making me want to strip naked and bathe.*

With a hand on her elbow, Rig steered Tavi toward a drinking establishment called Seven Angry Sisters.

Once inside, Tavi could see why the 'sisters' were angry. The place's stench was even worse than at the docks. Here, the malodor of sweat and unbathed people added a pungent aroma.

Tavi pulled the cloak over her nose, thankful for the spritz of orange blossom cologne she'd sprayed onto it in the morning.

Taller than most people, Rig glanced over the heads of the crowd. He bent and whispered in her ear, "Over there," and pointed to a dimly lit back corner. Rig pressed forward, his large frame cutting a path through the packed late-afternoon drinkers.

People stared at her and whispered as she passed. A few even sniggered and laughed behind their hands.

Tavi had never been on the receiving end of snickers or bullying behavior. She whispered to Rig, "Why are they staring and pointing at me?"

He chuckled. "Your nobility is obvious, Tavi."

"But I'm dressed like them."

"Yeah, well humble clothing can't hide the fact that you're clean, have well-groomed hair, and you smell nice," Rig said.

Tavi guffawed. "I supposed I should have dragged myself through horse shit before coming?"

"That would have helped," he said.

Rig didn't sound like he was joking.

As they neared the corner table, Tavi spied a small woman in the shadows of the booth's corner seat. A dingy cloak hood obscured her face.

She clutched a mug of ale in tiny hands. Though her clothes were frayed and unkempt, the woman's fingernails were clean and neatly trimmed.

Rig nodded to the seats beside the woman as he ducked to fit into the booth under the pub's sagging eaves. Tavi took the remaining seat, opposite Rig.

"Blessed be Night's Sister," Rig said.

"For sparing us a trip to the Well of Sorrows," Cleo said. She gave Rig a sideways glance, sipped her ale, then laughed.

Rig joined in her laughter, as if they were sharing a joke Tavi didn't understand.

"Always good to see you, Cleo. And thanks for meeting with us," Rig said. "This is Octavia di Māja Babesta, Mistress Fortunata's granddaughter." Rignar spoke low so only Octavia and Cleo could hear.

Cleo kept her eyes forward, giving Tavi not so much as a glance. "I know who she is." Her voice was strong and clear.

Just as Tavi was unused to being the subject of ridicule, she was also not accustomed to being ignored. She coughed, hoping to get Cleo's full attention, but Cleo continued to stare ahead as if pretending that Octavia wasn't even there.

Perhaps sensing the growing tension, Rig plowed ahead and began spelling out their plan. "I know you have a personal rule not to work for the Mājas—"

"'Cause they're all shite-eating wankers who'll put my arse on the line then leave me with my knickers down, cheeks flapping in the cold while they take care to have zero blow-back."

Tavi opened her mouth to protest the unfair generalization, but Rig shot her a glare and held up a hand to halt her from speaking. She wanted to reprimand him for impertinence but knew she wasn't in a place to chastise her vassal guard. Tavi held her tongue.

Rig continued. "I wouldn't ask this of you unless—"

"Unless you weren't shagging this rich tart holding your leash in one hand and your dick in the other?"

Tavi's eyes blazed with anger, but Rig laughed.

"You read me dead," he said.

Cleo chuckled too and wiped ale foam from her lips. She put two fingers in her mouth and gave a shrill whistle. A red-faced barmaid soon appeared, and Cleo merely held up two fingers. The barmaid gave a nod, apparently knowing exactly what that meant.

Octavia's cheeks still burned with anger when the barmaid returned and slammed two mugs onto the sticky table, ale sloshing out. Rig reached across, grabbed a mug, and downed nearly the entire thing in one gulp.

Seeing both Cleo and Octavia raise their brows at him, he shrugged.

"Since the trials, I can't get drunk even if I try," Rig said.

"Then you're not trying hard enough." Cleo raised her mug.

They clinked cups and drank, oblivious of Tavi. She sipped the bitter ale. It was too warm and skunky, but at least it was wet.

After a few moments of silent drinking, Cleo said, "I'm willing to break my rule for you because of what you did for me. I do this, Rig, and we're even, yes? No more favors owed between us?"

"Yep."

Cleo pushed back her cowl and glanced at Octavia and looked Tavi up and down as if appraising her. "Not my type, but I can see the attraction." Cleo sniffed. "And smells like Parthinian gold, and I don't mean the wine. You're getting paid handsomely too, huh?"

"You could say that," Rig said. He glanced over his mug at Tavi.

Cleo noticed the exchange. "Okay, now I gotta know what she's paying you so I can name my price."

Tavi started to tell the locks expert that it was none of her damned business what she was paying Rig, but he interrupted her again.

"Not being paid in Parthinians, Cleo." He caught her eye. "My fee is something far more valuable to me."

Cleo's already saucer-like eyes grew wider. She glanced at Tavi, then back at Rig to gauge the truth of what he implied. Finally, she spoke to Tavi. "You would do that? Do you even have the power to—I mean only a..."

Her voice trailed off as she seemed to piece together the threads of their as-yet-to-be-revealed plot.

"Don't tell me you aim to purloin a…" Cleo glanced around and then lowered her voice. "You want to steal a Domanulos?"

Both Octavia and Rignar nodded.

Cleo let out a long, thin whistle between her teeth and settled back into her seat. She downed the rest of her ale, and this time Rig called for more.

After a few moments of silent thinking, Cleo asked, "Please tell me you're going after Batiste." Her eyes glistened with the fire of hope.

Tavi merely nodded.

"Why do you ask?" Rig said.

The zealous glint disappeared from her eyes, and her expression turned dour. Her words came out clipped. "That pig-fucking bastard's reputation extends beyond the hallowed halls of Babesta."

She directed her next words to Tavi. "Down here at the bottom of the hill, people hate you folks from the Mājas. Not that I expect you to know that 'cause you ain't got nothing to do with common folks."

Tavi didn't know that. She didn't interrupt, though, and listened as Cleo continued.

"So, when I tell you that Batiste is the most hated prig of all you Māja folk, you gotta know that's a feat 'cause down here in the Shills, we hate all you wankers behind the walls."

Cleo took a long draw of her ale and, noticing the disbelieving look on Octavia's face, shrugged. "Maybe hard to hear, but it's the truth."

Tavi sipped the piss water from the chipped mug but remained silent. *I need to learn why they hate us so much. I mean, without us, they'd have nothing. Are they just jealous?*

The barmaid arrived with two more mugs, and Cleo and Rig grabbed them.

Tavi finally spoke. "Yes, my uncle Batiste is the target. Can we count on you, then, to be our key? Will you join our Sigil Five and help us liberate the Domanulos from my foul uncle's hand?"

Cleo raised her mug again. "Here's to ridding the world of that prig's stench."

They clanked mugs, and the three toasted her uncle's demise. *I hope I never again toast someone's death.*

Putting her mug down, Tavi said, "I cannot argue against your sentiment. I hadn't known my uncle's reputation for odious actions spread beyond the confines of Babesta." *Though it does not surprise me. Men with such predatory appetites often seek satisfaction of their depraved desires anywhere they can easily attain victims.*

Tavi continued. "I only hope you, Cleo, are up to the task. No offense—I'm sure you are a skilled lock pick. But our mark will not be found in a humble Shills establishment." Tavi wrinkled her nose as she glanced around the Seven Angry Sisters. "We are infiltrating a Māja compound. And Batiste, as a first-in-line successor—and having made many enemies—has extra tight security measures. My cousin, Gavino, says Batiste uses enchanted locks and traps crafted by Artifexa mages. I can't imagine you have experience with such things."

Cleo and Rig exchanged a look, and Cleo grinned. "No, I don't suppose *you* could imagine that." She sipped her ale and then said, "Would it make you feel better—more trusting—if I told you I was once a member of Māja Artifexa?"

Tavi raised an eyebrow. "Were you?"

Cleo snorted. "No."

Rig and Cleo both gave a hearty laugh, but Tavi didn't find the joke funny.

"Look, do you got anyone else to risk their ass for this?" Cleo asked.

Octavia sighed. "No. You may find this difficult to believe, but I don't know people who tout 'breaking and entering' as a skill."

"No, don't 'spose you do," Cleo said.

"I understand your trepidation about risking your freedom, or life, for this cause, but I don't want to risk mine—or Rig's either—if we don't have a solid plan with capable people. If this is to work, each member of the Sigil Five must be top notch."

"And 'cause I'm from the Shills, I can't be top notch? That's what you're sayin'?"

Tavi mumbled a protest.

Cleo cut in. "I know your type. Been locked behind a stone wall your whole life and don't know a Sicara's damned thing 'bout what's outside that lovely prison."

Tavi wanted to protest but realized she couldn't. What Cleo said was true. Tavi had never been to the Shills before this day, and Rig was the only person she'd ever met from outside Māja walls.

"Maybe I was born in the Shills, but my lineage is magic folk, and I trained with an old Artifexa lock master. The one who taught all them fancy Artifexa folk on that grand hill of yours about how to enchant them locks."

Cleo beamed with obvious pride.

"Is this true?" Tavi asked. She directed her question to Rig.

He nodded.

"Course it's true," Cleo said. "I may be poor and dirty, but I don't lie. Yeah, I did jobs for Mājas. Wix and even Soldista, see. Lots of times with my old mentor as a guide. But on the last job I did for a Māja, they got the goods, and I got this."

Cleo turned her head so Octavia could see the now-silvery scar from a gash across the right side of her face, from her eyebrow to her cheekbone.

With smooth pale skin, wide amber-brown eyes, and red-stained lips that formed a perfect pout, Cleo had been beautiful before being marred by the ugly scar.

Cleo pulled the cowl back over her head, stood, and plunked a Parthinian silver onto the still-wet table. "I'm in, if you still want to work with a lowly Shills girl. My fee will be exorbitant, but if you pull this off, you can afford it."

Octavia rose too and extended her hand. "Then welcome to the Sigil Five."

Chapter Five

True to his promise, Gavino secured the services of Sabine the Ember Dancer to distract Batiste on the night of the heist. Tavi had never met Sabine, and though she wanted to trust Gavino, Tavi decided their entire team should meet to review the plan before the night of Batiste's last birthday.

They could not, however, meet again in her solar. Cleo appearing within Babesta walls would get the entire Māja's tongues wagging. Meeting again in the Shills would also be risky. All the Mājas paid little "mice" to watch and report. If Tavi, Junia, and Gavino breezed into the Shills, by the time they left, every Cordomis of each Māja would call a meeting about it.

Again, Rig provided the solution. "There is a little-known place," he said. "Dirty, smelly, and not fit for noble people like you and Junia, but it will be private."

"I notice you didn't include Gavino in your description of lofty folk," Tavi said.

"You know where Gavino spends his time. Would you call him noble?"

Tavi couldn't disagree. Her cousin spent more time outside the walls of the Māja district than inside them. "Let us proceed with getting word to the rest of the Sigil Five."

A few days later, Rig guided Tavi through a maze of underground tunnels winding through the damp earth underneath Partha. She knew such tunnels existed but had never been in them.

Dark and dank, Rig carried a lantern in one hand while holding her hand in the other. Rats and roaches scurried. The sound made Tavi's skin crawl. *I will need two baths after this.*

They walked for what seemed like forever. Finally, the musty air gained a fresh odor: The sea.

Their final destination was a cave the sea had carved into the limestone cliffs south of Partha overlooking the Straits of Minea. The sound of crashing waves and the call of seabirds echoed off the cave's walls.

People had dragged large stones into a semicircle at the cave's edge. Close enough to the edge to gather light, but far enough back to avoid tumbling over the edge to a swift death.

Tavi pulled her woolen cloak tighter, glad that Rig had suggested the extra layer for warmth. "I didn't know this existed. Why would someone bother tunneling to this cave?"

Rig shrugged. "Not sure, exactly. My master, Mordranis, showed it to me. Said it had been here as long as anyone knew." He placed the lantern on a stone with a flattened top. "The others should arrive soon."

"Let us hope." Tavi wrapped her arms around herself, trying to keep warm in the damp sea air. The Māja compounds were situated high atop the hills of Partha where the sea's mists burned off in the early morning light of the two suns. She was rarely chilly in Partha.

Cleo soon arrived, her diminutive figure decked out in dark brown leather pants, boots, and gloves, and wrapped in a dark emerald-green cloak that contrasted with her auburn hair. She said little and took up position at the wall near the cave's edge, staring down at the roiling waves.

Gavino's boisterous prattling preceded him. His voice echoed off the walls of the earthen tunnel. Tavi was relieved they'd followed Rig's suggestion for meeting so far from Partha, especially since her cousin seemed incapable of lowering his volume.

Tavi had expected Junia to accompany Gavino and Sabine, but Gavino arrived with only one woman.

As if expecting her question, Gavino said, "My dear sister Junia sends her apologies, but our father has tasked her with something important that drew her attention today. She assures me, though, that all is falling into place for a spectacular celebration for our dear uncle Batiste's birthday. And yes, he has graciously accepted Junia's gift of a fête in his honor."

Tavi clapped. "That is good news, Gavino. It would have killed our current plan if dear uncle decided he didn't want a celebration in his honor."

"According to Junia, Batiste was wary of her suggestion. No doubt questioning the intentions of one of his sister Eligia's children doing something nice for him."

"As he should," Tavi said. "Junia throwing a party for Batiste? It should raise his suspicion.

Did he agree only to plan a plot of his own? A counter-attack?"

Gavino stroked his beard as he considered it. "Perhaps. But when Junia suggested it was my idea—to strengthen ties within our house in opposition to Wix—he changed his tone." Gavino gestured toward the woman who'd accompanied him. "And when Junia told him I'd secured one of Qülla's most celebrated ember dancers as a gift? Well, he was all ears after that."

"Like a fat rat lured to a cheese wheel," Cleo said.

"Are you calling me a cheese?" the woman with Gavino asked.

They all chuckled, and Tavi extended a thin hand to her. "Sabine, I presume."

Sabine proffered a hand gloved in the finest pale ivory dreyskin, a red woolen cowl obscuring her face in shadow. She had a melodic Qülla accent. "I am Sabine. A pleasure to meet you."

"Good to see you again, Sabine," Cleo said.

Sabine released her hand from Tavi's grip and went to Cleo. She removed her cowl, revealing a wave of lustrous black hair cascading down her back. Sabine kissed Cleo on each cheek and then embraced her and whispered something in her ear that Tavi couldn't hear.

Cleo laughed heartily as the women parted.

"I didn't know you two knew each other," Tavi said.

"Oh, you know, all us lowly people from outside the Mājas know each other," Cleo said.

The way Cleo spoke, Tavi couldn't tell if the woman was joking or not. Rig laughed, but when Tavi shot him a glare, he wiped the mirth from his face.

"Your reputation for being one of the finest ember dancers precedes you, Sabine. My dear cousin believes your hip swirling is so good, it will be enough to distract my odious uncle while we—liberate—his Domanulos. Please excuse my, perhaps, rather ignorant question, but what about the ember dance makes it so irresistible?"

Cleo rolled her eyes, and Gavino guffawed, but Sabine did not show any offense at the question.

"It is not ignorant to ask questions about something you do not understand," Sabine said. She gave Cleo a reproachful look, then continued. "I assume, then, that you have not experienced the ember dance?"

Tavi shook her head.

Sabine sat on a stone and gestured for the others to join her. She moved like vapor escaping a smoking vestibule. "I cannot divulge the deepest secrets of the dance for its origins are sacred, and a gift from Lumine."

"The moon goddess of Indrasi?" Tavi said.

Sabine nodded once and blinked slowly, her long, silky black eyelashes brushing her cheek. "The Sister's grace flows through me when I dance, you see, and her secrets I am bound to keep."

Tavi shook her head. "I honestly do not even know what that means." The lack of an answer frustrated her. "How is some sacred moon goddess dance supposed to lure Uncle into a state of unguarded ease?"

Sabine rose, removed her cloak, and took up position in front of Tavi. At first, she merely focused her gaze on Tavi, looking so intently into her eyes, Tavi shifted with discomfort.

It is like this woman sees through me to the depths of my innermost self.

Without moving from her spot or shifting her gaze away from Tavi, Sabine began by winding her arms upward, her movements fluid. Next, she swayed gently from the shoulders, her hair a waterfall of shiny black.

Though Tavi had never had amorous feelings toward the feminine, the heat of passion rose within her. Her neck flushed.

Within a few minutes, Sabine's slow, undulating dance reached her hips. While she kept her feet planted, Sabine's body moved to a rhythm only she heard, but everyone in the cave felt. Not once did she take her eyes off Tavi.

Her face flushed, and Tavi's breath caught in her throat.

Gavino coughed. "You best cease your dance, dear Sabine, before you make my cousin enrapture herself right here and now."

Sabine smiled and slowly wound down her miraculous movement. "Now, friend, do you understand? When one is gifted the ember dance, they are being given the gift of desire focused entirely on them. If two people stare into each other's eyes long enough, they might fall in love." She winked.

"I see," Tavi said. She pushed her cowl back from her neck, thankful now for the cool sea air. "But you don't…"

Sabine tsked. "No. Of course not. That is forbidden. Part of the allure though, you see. The recipient of the dance can feast with their eyes and all senses except touch." Sabine wrapped herself in her cloak and sat. "In Qülla, it is against the law to touch an ember dancer."

"People are thrown into prison for touching you?" Tavi asked.

Sabine shook her head. "Oh no. Not prison. Exalted Sunya di Kovan has mandated that anyone touching an ember dancer loses whatever portion of their body defiled the dancer."

Tavi gulped.

"What is the point of the seductive dance, if the recipient of the gift cannot—how to say this—reap the benefits of their heightened feelings?" Tavi asked.

Sabine gave her a languid smile. "The ember dance stokes the fires. What one does with the glowing embers... Well, that is up to them."

"Sabine has performed in Exalted Sunya's court," Gavino said. "She and her two sisters are favorites the Kovan Dynasty court."

Sabine merely nodded.

"You perform this dance at court? In front of a large gathering?" Tavi tsked. "Then what? They have an orgy?"

Sabine shrugged. "I could not say. I merely dance. What happens after I leave the stage is not for me to know."

"The southern city has odd customs," Cleo said.

On this, Tavi could agree with their locks expert.

"I have been to Qülla," Gavino said. "And I had the great honor of attending a fête at the Palace di Soli. They served only the finest Bardivian wines, and the food was beyond compare. The dancers and entertainment? As fine as any we have in Partha. Qülla is a seductive place, and nowhere do you see this more than in the Palace di Soli. But I can assure you, cousin, there are no orgies there."

"Who gives a sea hag's hairy banch who and when rich folk are bangin' in a southern city. Are we going to steal a ring or not?" Cleo asked.

They all laughed.

"Point taken," Gavino said. "As the tactician for this caper, I've created detailed instructions for each of you. You will study these here, and then we will destroy them before we go."

Gavino handed each of them a rolled, sealed parchment with a unique color and symbol. Tavi's color was purple, and the symbol on the wax seal was a masquerade mask.

"It's lovely, Gavino. I hate to break this seal," Tavi said.

As she spoke, Cleo and Rignar each unceremoniously broke the seals on their documents and began reading. Tavi was about to ask about their symbols, but as she unfurled her paper, she saw five symbols scrawled at the top of the page.

Her symbol—the mask—came first, followed by a dagger. She glanced up at Rig, his eyes busy devouring his instructions. Yes, the dagger was a fitting symbol for the blade of their crew.

The next symbol was a ladies' fan. Tavi guessed it represented Sabine, the ember dancer and seductive distraction. The last two symbols were a key—obviously for their locksmith, Cleo—and the last was an hourglass. Tavi supposed the timepiece represented Gavino, the planner and master of time for the heist.

Beneath the symbols, Gavino had penned, "The Sigil Five." Tavi liked the sound of it, and her heart raced with the thrill of anticipation at thrusting herself into danger.

Until the night of Batiste's birthday, Tavi's job was to help plan and to be the bankroll for their robbery. She'd been curious about what specifically Gavino would have her do the night of the actual heist.

While the others studied pages filled with detailed notes, Tavi's page was nearly empty. It said only this:

"Dearest Cousin, you have only two things you must do this night. First, remain sober.

Difficult, I know, when in Uncle's company. For securing the optimal opportunity for the Batiste's Domanulos to transfer its power, the intended recipient must be free of clouded mind. At least this is what my Artifexa spellcraft expert told me.

"The only other job for you is to be in dear uncle's private quarters at the time of his death. You will accompany Rig. Though he is your vassal and at your command, on this one night, Tavi, you must be at his command. When his blade draws out Batiste's last breath, *you* must be the one to take the Domanulos from his finger. If you are not present at the precise moment of his death, the entire scheme will be for naught."

Though her page had fewer words than the rest, what Gavino said sobered her. *We are truly going to kill a man*. She wondered if the others thought of this too.

For his part, death was not new to Rig. Fen Menir, the house of assassins and spies, had raised him. He'd taken vows to Sicara, the goddess of death, and was beholden to bring souls to her. Tavi didn't know how many people he'd killed in his relatively young life, but she knew his blade had been wet with blood before.

Tavi glanced at Cleo, still fixated on the parchment she'd received. Cleo was an Artifexa-trained locksmith but had lived in the Shills most of her life. It was possible that Cleo had known death.

Gavino, too, was more experienced in the world—and the games of the Mājas—than Tavi. Who was to say how many lives he'd been responsible for snuffing out. Not as the actual killer, per se, but the one who placed an order for death. *That is the way of the Mājas. Dirty another's hands with such work. But doesn't it still tarnish one's soul, even if my hands do not actually do the killing? In the eyes of the gods, will I be a killer too, even if it is Rig's blade that ends Batiste's life?*

Before her conscious overrode her resolve, Tavi reminded herself of Batiste's many sins against others. She'd tried to scrub her mind of the memory of Batiste pressing himself into her, attempting to take what she did not freely consent to give. *If father hadn't walked into the room at that moment…*

Tavi shuddered. *If ever a man deserved vigilante-style justice, it is Batiste.* Her resolve would not waver ever again.

Rig had been quiet but broke the cave's silence with a question. "You are certain that old Gerard is still Batiste's private guard? That he will be the Fen Menir brother assigned to watch Batiste's private quarters that night?"

"Quite certain," Gavino said. "Gerard has been Batiste's private guard for over a year now, and it is rumored that they drink together in some of the roughest ale houses in the Shills."

Rig nodded. "I have heard that as well." He glanced around, as if unsure he should say what he wanted to.

"What else?" Tavi asked.

He let out a sigh. "This could just be a specious rumor created by his enemies. You know, as the Mājas do."

"What could be worse than what people already say about him?" Cleo asked.

Rig nodded. "True."

Tavi gave her hand a rolling motion. "Out with it then. You can't cast a line then reel it back without having caught a fish."

Rig chuckled. "Agreed. Look, if the rumors are true, Batiste's hungers are no longer satiated by mere pleasure of the flesh. People say his appetites have taken an even darker turn, and that he derives pleasure from observing Gerard send souls to Sicara."

Tavi's lip curled in disgust, as did Cleo's.

"What a sick dung-licking butt boil," Cleo said.

Gavino laughed. "What colorful phrasing." He clapped. "Could not have said it better myself. I want to go drinking with this one."

Cleo gave him a look that let him know she would never accompany him to an alehouse.

Sabine had been quiet, but this new information about Batiste had made her blanch. "If this is true…" Her eyes found Rig's and pleaded. "You will arrive in time, right? Before I was worried only that he'd try to despoil me, but what if…"

Rig's look was intense. "I vow to you, Sabine. I will not allow this man to rob you of life or dignity." His hand found the hilt of the Vandu blade. "Batiste's next birthday will be his last."

The intensity of his eyes, the hard set of his jaw, Tavi knew were evidence of his resolve. She did not doubt him.

Sabine's expression softened, and she gave Rig a single nod. "I trust in your blade then, Ser Assassin. My life is in your hands."

Gavino steered them back to the plan, and they ran through it several times. He took turns quizzing each about their respective jobs and the timing for each moment of the night's journey.

Before they parted, he lit a fire in the center of their semicircle where the remnants of prior fires remained. They each dropped their parchment notes into the fire and silently watched as they turned to ash.

"It is done," Rig said. "The fire binds us, and the smoke carries our plan to the ears of the gods."

"Let us hope they are listening," Gavino said.

"And that no one here has given any of them cause to find our scheme more offensive than letting that puss-filled sore to live," Cleo said.

"Blessings of the gods to the Sigil Five, then," Tavi said. The gathered repeated Tavi's prayer for blessings, then departed the dank cave and returned to the light of the two brothers.

CHAPTER SIX

Tavi arrived with her family at Batiste's birthday fête an hour late. Arriving at the time stated in the invite would be seen as extremely uncharacteristic, especially for anyone on or related to members of the house's Cordomis. The first guests to arrive had been far-flung relatives, tied to the Babesta Māja by the thinnest of threads. An honored guest at a Babesta gathering normally doesn't begin accepting toasts until all members of the Cordomis arrive. But Batiste was already sporting red, flushed cheeks and slurred speech.

Good, Tavi thought. She cast a glance back at Rig, and he gave her a slight, nearly imperceptible nod to reassure her. *Thank the gods I have him by my side tonight. I could not go through with this without him.*

Servants silently swooped by with wine goblets. Tavi was glad the party was taking place at the compound of her cousins Junia and Gavino. They served much better wine than Batiste.

As soon as a servant tendered her a goblet, Tavi's mother, Hortencia, grabbed Tavi's father and pushed through the throng. Her mother no doubt sought her aunt Eligia, Gavino and Junia's mother and second in line to succeed Fortunata as head of the Cordomis.

Tavi's older brother, Silvino, whispered in her ear. "Mother so likes to keep Eligia in her good graces, doesn't she."

They watched their parents disappear into the crowd. Tavi agreed with Silvino. "She likes to keep father's friends close."

Silvino raised a cup. "And his enemies even closer." He gave her a wink. "Enjoy this ridiculous attempt by Junia to make peace among our kin."

Tavi so wanted to set him straight about the party's true purpose, but she couldn't risk confiding the details, even to her much-loved brother.

Tavi searched the gathering for Junia or Gavino, but spied neither.

Panic welled. *Have they abandoned this farce?*

She whispered to Rig. "Do you see our friends?"

Rig scanned the room and gave a head bob to someone he saw, but Tavi couldn't. "Gavino is making his way over."

Remaining at Tavi's back, Rig stood with arms crossed and took up the stance of alert readiness. Gavino soon arrived, a plate of skewered fruits and spice-dusted nuts in his hand.

He greeted Tavi with a kiss on each cheek, then a light peck on the lips. "Dear cousin." Taking her hand, he pressed back from her and took in her attire. "Let me have a look at you. Who designed your look? Ser Silveri?"

They continued with the exchange of mutual adulation as any onlookers expected of them, then Gavino sidled closer. "Batiste is performing his part admirably tonight." His voice dripped with sarcasm.

"The one thing we can count on. Uncle will feed his appetites well," Tavi said. "And what of your sister? I hoped to see her before the hour grows late."

Gavino ate an entire fruit skewer in one bite. "It's her party, Tavi. She's playing hostess. The last I saw, she was speaking with grandmother."

Tavi raised an eyebrow. "Fortunata is here?"

Gavino tittered. "You didn't think she'd miss her own son's birthday fête?"

"I suppose not." Because of the farcical nature of this birthday party, Tavi kept forgetting that those outside the Sigil Five didn't know the party was a sham.

"And what about dear uncle's gift? Is that package wrapped and ready for delivery?" Tavi asked.

Gavino chuckled. "By Sicara's bloody teats, Tavi, once this night is through, you need to cut with the attempt at sly conversation."

Tavi didn't return the mirth. Her nerves were too frayed for verbal jousting with Gavino. "Just answer the question."

"Yes. Batiste's 'gift' is in a safe location and will be presented to Batiste when I give the signal to Junia."

"And when will that be exactly?" Tavi asked.

"When it looks like Batiste is so deep in his cups that his guard is ready to trundle him home."

To Tavi, that didn't seem far off.

She sipped the wine, and Gavino put a hand on hers. "Remember your rule number one for the evening."

Tavi let out a sigh but halted her drink. She was glad of Gavino's reminder to remain sober. Getting tipsy could endanger their plans, and she had to ensure the highest potential for the evening's desired outcome.

An hour passed, and then nearly two. Tavi saw Junia only in passing, but her cousin gave a wink and a reassuring nod. As drunk as Batiste seemed when they arrived, she expected that he'd have received his parting 'gift' at least an hour ago. But Batiste remained, soaking up the attention like a parched sea sponge accepting water.

Finally, Junia made her way to the front of the grand room where the musical performers were seated. She asked them to pause, and she raised her voice. "Time for presentation of a gift."

A few people noticed, but mostly the wine-filled partygoers ignored her. Gavino pressed forward to help his sister and whistled loudly.

Getting their attention, he shouted, "Junia has a special gift for our dear uncle."

Junia put out her hand, inviting Batiste to step forward. He laughed, took her hand, and planted a sloppy kiss on it. "A present for your old uncle. Why, I have everything a man could want, child."

His eyes held hers a bit too long. Tavi's skin crawled. She imagined Junia would later wash her hand raw where the old letch had placed his rancid lips.

Junia spoke loudly so that the crowd could hear. "Oh, this you do not have. Arriving recently from the fair city to our south, a unique offering of friendship, Uncle."

She gestured to the doorway of the hall leading downstairs to the kitchens. A small woman wrapped in a cloak of vibrant red with orange embroidered suns glided toward them.

Sabine wore no jewels, and she hadn't applied the heavy makeup often worn by performers or dancers. Her only makeup was black kohl liner to highlight her eyes, and vibrant red lip paint that matched her cloak.

As she approached Junia and Batiste, Sabine gave a low bow, outstretching one arm in a graceful curve, her body bowed but her eyes latching onto Batiste's.

Batiste's expression shifted from bemusement to genuine awe.

"I present to you, Sabine of Qülla, a famed ember dancer who most recently performed for the court of Exalted Sunya di Kovan. She, Uncle, is my gift to you. A private ember dance for one."

Batiste was uncharacteristically speechless. His eyes remained locked with Sabine's.

"Stare into anyone's eyes long enough, and they will fall in love with you," Sabine had said. Sabine has him in her grasp, Tavi thought.

When Batiste said nothing but merely stared at Sabine, Junia said, "What say you, Uncle? Do you accept my gift?"

Batiste finally found his words, but his eyes remained glued on Sabine's. "Accept it? Why dear Junia, this is the most welcome gift anyone has ever given me. I mark what you proffered tonight and accept the unifying vow of friendship within our house."

Having said the expected words of gratitude for such a generous gift, the crowd cheered and shouted self-serving praise to Māja Babesta.

Mistress Fortunata, seated on the seat of honor at the head of the room, leaned on her cane and stood. She gave Junia a contemptuous look, then sidled from the room, her guards trailing behind.

Tavi turned to Rig. "What do you make of that?" she whispered.

He shrugged, but said, "Perhaps she knows his reputation, and is repulsed that Junia gave Batiste a gift that all should know he'll abuse."

Rig perhaps had the right of it. Tavi only hoped that when the sun rose and Sabine was safe while Batiste lay dead that Mistress Fortunata would approve of the gift after all.

Rig whispered into Tavi's ear. "I must leave now to meet Cleo. Remember, once Batiste has left, head with Gavino to his compound. He'll lead you to the wall on the south side. I will meet you there."

Tavi nodded, and Rig disappeared into the crowd. He'd accompanied her nearly everywhere and at all times for most of the past year. Rig had become like a second shadow, but considerably warmer. His absence felt like she'd lost an appendage. *It is likely unwise to have allowed someone to become such a necessary requirement for my happiness.*

Practically salivating, Batiste then announced he was retiring to his compound to 'enjoy' Junia's generous gift. Tavi expected old Gerard, Batiste's usual personal guard, to step forward. Both Gavino and Rig had reported that Gerard, who enjoyed the fruit of the vine as much as Batiste, was still assigned by Fen Menir as Batiste's personal guard.

But Gerard was nowhere to be seen. Instead, a retinue of three guards stepped forward from the shadows to accompany her uncle. And one of them had his hand on the hilt of a Vandu blade.

Gavino and Junia still stood near Batiste. As they saw the same thing Tavi did, their eyes grew wide with surprise. She couldn't hear them but could read Gavino's lips. "Fuck," he said under his breath.

Tavi couldn't agree more with the sentiment. They hadn't anticipated Rig going against three Fen Menir trained guards, and one an older and more experienced Vandu.

Tavi's instinct was to call the plan off. This was a sign from the gods to abandon the quest. Rig couldn't cut his way through Batiste's guard. Fen Menir rules required that he never kill a brother of Fen Menir unless their leader ordered it. *If he kills three? They will make him pay with his life.*

Tavi might distract two of the guards with drink, and the sleeping draught Gavino had procured for her. But the third guard, the one with his hand on the hilt of the green Vandu blade…

Impervious to poisons. And since his Vandu trials, Rig struggles even to get drunk.

Yes, abandoning the plan was the best course of action. She moved through the crowd, heading to Junia and Gavino to sound the alarm.

But as Batiste exited the room, Sabine cast a glance back at them. The look in her eyes reminded Tavi of the Sigil Five's promise to Sabine. And Tavi couldn't stop thinking about what Gavino had told them about how Batiste's appetites had grown even darker in recent years.

We cannot abandon Sabine, or she might not live to see tomorrow.

Junia asked, "What now?"

"Gavino and I meet Rig as planned," Tavi said.

"But—"

Tavi cut her off. "We cannot abandon Sabine."

Gavino let out a loud breath. "There will be a high price paid for this reward."

The thought made Tavi tremble. "I cannot allow…" She didn't need to finish the sentence. They were all concerned about the same thing.

Finally, she said, "Let us go, Gavino. We must not keep our friends waiting."

On their brisk walk to Batiste's compound, Tavi mulled over her next move. She must decide whether she would warn Rig by telling him the truth, or keep the new information secret, thus potentially forcing him into a trap that would test his loyalties. *How deep is his love for me, truly?* Tavi wondered. *Will he go against vows made to Night's Sister and his brotherhood to remain by my side?*

She had only minutes to decide whether she would put him to this test.

Chapter Seven

Moonlight shone on Rig's pale hair, making him look like an apparition in the eerie late-hour darkness. He stood by the rear wall of Batiste's compound, but Cleo was nowhere in sight.

Gavino's voice was airy as he huffed to catch his breath after the near-run to meet them. "Where is the Key?"

"She's inside, eliminating the first barrier," Rig said.

As Rignar talked, he removed a steel grate from the wall. Intended to secure the sewer tunnels of Batiste's compound from interlopers, someone had severed the steel from its foundation.

"After you," Rig said to Gavino. "Follow your cousin, Tavi, and I will have your back."

Gavino appeared to know his way through the labyrinth of dirt-walled tunnels burrowed into the earth beneath Batiste's sprawling house.

"It's like you've done this before," Tavi said.

Her cousin tsked. "Of course I have. What, do you think I hadn't investigated every aspect of our plan?"

Tavi followed in silence and didn't reveal her thoughts for fear of causing Gavino offense. In truth, Gavino had so convincingly played the part of a young man whiling his days away drinking, seeking thrills inside pleasure dens, and spending his family's money, Tavi hadn't realized he was also competent.

Before long, Gavino led them down a path that glowed from a lamp's light. As they approached, Cleo said, "'Bout fuckin' time you lot got here."

Her cowl and knitted brows cast a deep shadow over her features making her look ominous. She stood next to a nondescript door with a simple lock that even a novice burglar could easily pick.

"You managed the barrier?" Gavino asked.

Cleo responded to his question with a glare that could melt steel. "Before we reach Batiste's private wing, we have another barrier then a poison trap. Rig, I'll need your help with that one."

He gave her a nod.

They stepped through the small doorway, remaining tight on Cleo's heels. They wound first right, then took a tunnel left toward another small doorway with a similar lock as the prior door. Nothing about the plain, wooden doorway warned that a magical ward protected it.

Tavi whispered to Gavino. "How can you tell which doors are warded?"

"*He* can't tell," Cleo answered. "That's why *I'm* here." Cleo paused near the door and held them back with an outstretched arm. "Now shut yer traps while I work. I gotta concentrate."

"I still don't understand," Tavi muttered.

Cleo paused and flashed an annoyed look. "I sense the magic." She rolled her eyes. "Gods preserve Babesta. Do you lot teach your people nothing about Artifexa?"

Tavi again felt the weight of her inexperience. She was so unlikely to ascend to the Cordomis, no one had bothered educating her about the workings of the other Mājas. Earlier in the evening she'd entered Batiste's party nervous about whether the other members of the Sigil Five were up to the task. Now, her concern shifted to her own competence not only to show herself worthy of the Domanulos, but of being ready for the power—and responsibility—it conferred.

As Cleo set about her work, Tavi remained still as glass, but her heart raced and her stomach roiled. They'd wasted no time working the plan, yet who could say how long Sabine could hold off Batiste's lecherous paws? *Make haste, Cleo,* Tavi thought.

With her diminutive hands outstretched and her eyes closed, Cleo examined the weaves of the magical ward. Tavi could no more imagine what Cleo sensed than she could sprout wings and fly. Cleo's brow creased, and her lips twisted in a grimace as though going through an unseen physical pain.

After a few moments of what looked like silent torture, she frowned one last time, then grinned. "Someone at Artifexa has finally learned a bi-element weave." She spun her hands and chanted words in Soligian, the ancient language of the mages. "I wonder who?" she whispered.

After a few moments of intense focus and quiet chants, Cleo released a deep breath and pronounced, "It is done."

Sweat matted stray hairs to her forehead, and her eyes looked tired. Gavino swept by her and opened the door without experiencing ill effect. Cleo wiped her brow and sipped from the water flask Rig handed her.

"Are you okay?" Tavi asked. "Do you have the strength to continue?" She couldn't help the worry seeping into her voice.

From the expression that washed over Cleo's face, you would think that Tavi had accused her of being a slint. Cleo wiped water from her mouth and handed the waterskin back to Rig. Giving Tavi only an angry glare for an answer, Cleo passed through the doorway and followed Gavino.

"I meant no offense," Tavi whispered to Rig.

He nodded and pointed toward the door, indicating she should continue on their path. Tavi also stepped over the threshold, Rig at her back. "Give it no thought, Tavi. Cleo is a professional and will do her job. Stay focused on our task, because I assure you she will."

The Sigil Five were proving their competency, making Tavi feel out of her element. Doubt crept in and plagued her. She had only one thing to do—to accept the Domanulos and hope that it accepted her. But with doubt about her worthiness—readiness even—to the task, she feared the Domanulos would deny her its power.

These doubts and more worried her as they made their way to the third and final tunnel doorway. As they approached another innocuous-appearing door, Cleo halted them at the edge of a dip in the dirt floor.

"Mark me well. Step a toe beyond this point, and you will not see the dawn." As she spoke, she tapped at the edge of the indent someone had made in the earth. "You're up, Vandu."

Rig stepped to Cleo's side and sighed. "Here's hoping my trials serve me." With his hand on the hilt of his Vandu blade, Rig whispered a prayer to Sicara and stepped forward, breeching the invisible barrier.

He'd moved only a few feet before reaching an unseen ward that triggered a poisonous greeting. Wooden panels on either side of the doorway dropped from hinges, opening their hidden compartments and releasing a noxious vapor with a hiss.

Rig took another step, and then another, creeping closer to the door. He didn't cough or sputter and showed no ill effects from the noxious vapor cloud hanging in the air. When he reached the door, Rig said, "Looks like they loaded only one batch."

Tavi released a sigh of relief that his Vandu trials had indeed made him impervious to poisons. Rig, too, looked relieved to have survived his first real-world test of immunity to the ill effects of poison.

"How will we know when it's safe to proceed?" Tavi asked.

She'd expected Cleo to answer, but Gavino chimed in. "As with the wards, Cleo can sense the residual magic that lingers. This spell, having been spent on Rig, will dissipate and release. She's waiting to sense it is gone."

Cleo neither agreed nor disagreed with Gavino, but kept a silent vigil, her look stern and focused on the doorway. After a time, she said, "The toxins are nearly gone, but a second trap was laid." Her voice was hoarse.

As with battling to thwart the prior ward, Cleo's forehead beaded with sweat. Her tiny body shook with effort against an invisible force.

"What type of ward?" Rig asked. "Is there anything I can do to assist?"

Tavi expected Cleo to say no or simply ignore Rig's question. She had thus far given the impression that she needed help from no one ever.

But to Tavi's surprise, Cleo croaked, her voice like a dried husk. "Weave a healing spell for me, Rig."

His eyes wide with surprise and confusion, Rig said, "I'm an assassin, Cleo, not a healer. I bring Sicara's kiss, not protect people from it. I don't know how to weave a healing spell."

Cleo's attention remained focused on an unseen enemy. A magical binding that appeared to be as strong as any iron lock. Her voice clipped, she snapped at him. "We don't have time to argue. You're surrounded by healing threads. Bind to one and thread it to me." She groaned in pain, then rasped, "Now!"

Rig, still looking confused, tried to do as he'd seen her do. He closed his eyes to concentrate, took a deep breath, and wound his hands. Rig whispered a prayer, but whether to Sicara, Mother of Death, or to another god, Tavi didn't know.

If Rig indeed cast a spell, Tavi could neither see nor sense it. After a few moments, Cleo's brow crease eased, and her trembling calmed.

Cleo hadn't defeated the magical lock yet, though. She and Rig continued their spells, each deeply focused on forces unseen and unknown to Tavi. After several moments, Cleo lowered her arms and pronounced the ward busted.

She swayed and nearly toppled, but Gavino caught her before she fell. "By the gods, what did you face here tonight?"

Cleo's eyes were sunken, and her lips dry, her skin even paler than before. She looked as though someone had sapped a decade of years from her. Though small, she had been a tiny bundle of nature's energy. Now, Cleo looked like a shattered seed.

"Will she be okay?" Tavi asked.

"I did what I could," Rig said. His voice carried the concern they all felt. He handed Gavino the waterskin.

Gavino trickled water onto her parched lips. "Drink, dear Cleo. You have performed your duty admirably, and I will see to it you are rightly rewarded for your efforts."

Still holding her in his arms, Gavino said, "Go ahead. I must tend to our Key. There will be no more wards or traps. Only guards to contend with in Batiste's private wing before reaching his inner chamber."

Tavi hesitated and twisted her cloak hem. "Will Cleo recover?"

Cleo spoke, her voice a barely audible whisper. "Go. Take the Domanulos so you have the Parthinians to pay my fee."

Gavino laughed. "Right she is." He put the waterskin to the Key's lips. "Do as she says, Tavi. Don't waste this opportunity." To Rig, Gavino said, "Remember the plan, Vandu. And no matter what happens in there, make sure you get Sabine and our Tavi out safely."

Rig said nothing but nodded toward the door. "Let's go, and stay tight on my heels."

Light on his feet for such a tall man, Rig made no sound as he navigated the dim corridors, hugging the walls like a shadow. Tavi followed on his heels, trying her best to be as quiet as Rig was.

He led them up a narrow back passageway leading to the upper floor of private rooms. As soon as they turned down a wide corridor leading toward the back of the house, they encountered their first potential roadblock.

Ahead, two guards stood at the entryway to Batiste's private quarters.

When laying out the plan, Gavino had said that the house guards would not be a problem. "I've paid one of the house servant's a fat sum to ply the guards with a celebratory wine cup in honor of their lord Batiste. Of course it will be laced with a sleeping draught, so you should encounter only men sleeping like babes on your way to Batiste's inner chambers."

These men were not sleeping. They whispered between themselves, and one chuckled softly at some private joke.

Rig cursed under his breath. "Fuck."

He pushed Tavi back against the wall and pressed his own back to the wall as well.

It took only a few moments for Tavi to realize why he was so upset. These were not house guards. *They are two of the men from Fen Menir who escorted Batiste home.* Men Tavi hadn't told Rig about.

"Is this a problem?" she whispered.

Rig didn't look at her, or answer. His hand reached for his blade hilt and rested there as if it could provide answers.

After a few minutes, Tavi said, "Rig? We can't keep Sabine waiting. What will you do?"

His jaw clenched, and he let out a long breath. Finally, he glanced down at her. "Do you promise you'll have my back? That you'll use the influence of your new station to intercede on my behalf with Fen Menir."

"Of course," Tavi said. It was the truth.

"Because what I'm about to do… They will issue a warrant for my death, Tavi. You understand?"

Her heart galloped wildly, and breath caught in her throat. If the Domanulos accepted her, she was about to become one of the most powerful people in Partha, a job she now realized she was quite ill-equipped for. She'd need Rig by her side in the future even more than in her past.

But that wasn't the complete story. Tavi loved him. She shouldn't have allowed herself to take Rignar as a lover in the first place, and she most certainly shouldn't have fallen in love with a servant indentured to her.

But she did love him, and the thought of losing him—to death or even circumstance—brought hot tears to her eyes.

"I promise," she said, and gave his hand a squeeze. "We're in this together, Rig. All the way to the end."

Rig smiled, pulled her close, and kissed her deeply. "To the end," he said, and it sounded more like a prayer than an oath.

Before she'd even opened her eyes, he was gone. She peeked around the corner, and as she did, the first man fell. Rig had slit his throat, and pink foam bubbled from the wide gash. *The work of his poisonous Vandu blade*, she thought.

Now approaching the second guard, the man had pulled a broadsword from his back. Though Rig was taller, the Fen Menir guard was older and more muscular. He held the sword in a defensive stance, and a smile curled his lip.

"By Sicara's bloody teat, Ser Nicandar was right. It *is* you who has plotted against the house."

The man's words seemed to take Rig off guard. He stopped cold and visibly blanched.

"That's right, Fen Menir knows. Batiste knows too." The guard's smile grew wider. "Yep, he's enjoying his 'gift.' Sicara will welcome two souls to the well tonight. The ember dancer's, and yours." He pointed at Rig with the tip of his sword. "Are you ready to meet Night's Sister?"

Rig had looked scared, but a new expression washed over him.

Resolve.

If the man wanted to live, he should not have mentioned Sabine dying. Rig seemed to give little care for his own life, but his vows of protection were sacred to him.

Rig gave the man a grin of his own as he raised his Vandu blade, eyeing it in the candlelight. The emerald green metal glinted, the dim light casting shadows on the blade's twisting engravings making them look like they moved.

"One nick, and you're done." Rig pointed his blade at the now-dead man on the floor behind him. "Ready to join your friend, then?"

The guard's smirk was gone, but his jaw twitched and he grunted as he thrust his massive blade forward. "Try to get a cut on me, whelp."

Rig danced away from the blow, rolled past the man, and came up with an uppercut across the back of his leg.

It was too dark to see if Rig injured the man. Rig sprung to his feet and spun to face his attacker before the guard could reset. *He has the agility of youth on his side,* Tavi thought.

The guard tried to spin, but he stumbled. His eyes wide, he got out one last garbled curse. "You feckin' traitor. You'll not get past Garsea."

With that, he fell to the floor. His legs jerked, and foam spewed from his open mouth. Soon, his eyes were glassy and vacant.

Before this night, I'd never seen a person die. Now I've witnessed two deaths.

Nausea washed over Tavi. She held her hand to her lips and swallowed hard, willing herself not to vomit. *And to think I'd planned to plunge my blade into a man's gut. I haven't the stomach for death.*

Rignar evinced no emotion about the dead man, but his Fen Menir brother's last words had spooked him. Rig glanced toward the doors leading to the inner chambers. "This is not good," he said. Rig wiped his blade clean on the dead man's shirt and rose as Tavi approached.

"What's wrong?"

"He mentioned Garsea." Rig sighed. "Garsea is the best Vandu in Fen Menir, and the personal guard to Master Nicandar, next in line to be Master of Fen Menir."

"And this is bad?"

Rig gave a wry laugh. "Bad? It's beyond bad, Tavi. Going against Garsea..." He shook his head. "Even if I somehow best him, the Mājas will never allow a house, even Babesta, to buy my exoneration for killing a Vandu."

Their plan was unraveling in real time. Blackness played at the edge of her vision, and slick sweat soaked her inner shirt. *Think, Tavi. Get it together. You haven't come this far to give up. What would Grandmother Fortunata do?*

As if Sicara herself delivered the thought to Tavi, she blurted out, "Then I will do it."

Rig gave her a condescending look.

He was about to speak, but Tavi cut him off. "You engage him while I will remain hidden. Wear him down. Maneuver him into position." Tavi pulled the dagger from the sleeve pocket where she'd hidden it. "You provide an opportunity and distraction, and I'll sink my blade into him."

Rig eyed the blade, his jaw again set and twitching. "By Sicara, you will be the death of me, won't you?"

Tavi stood on tiptoes and kissed Rig. "To the end."

Chapter Eight

Rig opened the ornately carved double doors leading to Batiste's solar and silently stepped inside. The room was dark except for a single lamp on the center table. On the opposite side of the round room, another set of doors led to Batiste's private bedchamber.

To Sabine.

Even darker than the corridor where two members of Fen Menir lay dead, Tavi's eyes had to adjust to the dim light.

A voice came from the shadows. "Ser Mordranis vouched for you." The man spat the words with venom. "Vouched for your feckin' hide while you trampled on your vows. On all Fen Menir has given you. And for what?"

Garsea stepped out of the shadows, revealing a man nearly Rig's height and arms corded with muscle. His black brows and neatly trimmed beard matched the color of the black cloak he removed and placed neatly on the large table at the room's center.

Rig said nothing in response but gently tapped Tavi with his foot, hinting for her to press back into the hall. Tavi did just that and pressed herself against the wall just outside the door. She closed her eyes and tried to calm her breath so she wouldn't reveal herself.

Rig unsheathed his dagger from the leather scabbard at his hip. No longer concealing his presence, Rig didn't bother to step lightly as he pressed forward into Batiste's solar.

It sounded like the men were circling, neither committing to an attack. Finally, Rig spoke.

"All Fen Menir has given me? You mean depriving me of family and home?"

Garsea laughed. "Oh, you mean the 'oh so loving' woman you called mother? How many Parthinians did Mordranis drop in her hand before she pushed you out the door, hmm? All too happy to be rid of one more hungry maw."

Rig didn't respond.

Tavi didn't know if Garsea spoke truthfully. Rignar never spoke of his past, and Tavi hadn't asked. She'd proclaimed love for him—'to the end'—and hadn't even known he'd been sold into indentured service.

I'm such a fool.

Garsea continued goading. "Took you from a cozy home, huh? That one dank room housing what? Four, maybe five other kids?"

"You know nothing about me," Rig spat.

Garsea chuckled. "Oh, I think I do. Haven't you figured it out yet? I *am* you. All brothers of Fen Menir began like you. Orphans of circumstance, rescued from a life of poverty and ruin to become esteemed members of Parthinian society."

Rig gave a wry laugh. "Esteemed? Then why do we wear invisible collars and leashes? Hmm?"

"Because we're dangerous, you twat. Besides, these Māja folks have so-called freedom. And what do they do with it? Live inside walled compounds, afraid to even leave their rooms for fear they'll be stabbed or eat food because it might be poisoned. If that's freedom, no thank you."

"Those are only two choices?" Rig snorted. "Maybe, just maybe, there's something else. People who sail the open seas. Family groups roaming the Sulmére desert. Hell, even commons shopkeepers get more out of life than Fen Menir masters or the so-called nobles living in the Mājas."

His voice held a tone she'd never heard from him before. It revealed the disdain he felt for the Mājas. By extension, it felt like an attack on her as well. *Could he truly love me when he seems to despise everything about my family and way of life?*

Garsea was quiet, and the two continued circling. Finally, Garsea shoved the table out of the way, wood scraping against wood.

"Come, boy. I promised to bring a soul to Sicara's well this night. Let us not keep Night's Sister waiting."

Tavi heard loud footfalls and a grunt. She hunkered down and peered through the slit between the wall and the door.

Garsea's back to her, Rig's blade-wielding hand already seeped crimson. His cloak, too, had been placed on the table, and he'd pulled his hair back into a leather tie. Rig always wore a mask of confidence, concealing any fear or doubt.

That mask had slipped. As he faced Garsea, Tavi saw for the first time the young man he truly was rather than the experienced assassin he projected himself to be. Worry for him swelled.

Garsea lashed out again, and Rig danced away from his blade this time, narrowly avoiding another cut. Though he was impervious to the deleterious effect of Garsea's Vandu blade, Garsea could still kill him by landing a fatal cut.

Tavi watched with growing dread as the two men fought, each knowing only one would survive the fight. Garsea thrust, sliced, and pressed into Rig, over and over. For his part, Rig took no part in attacking but played a game of defense. He danced and blocked, rolled away and deflected, but also took cut after cut.

A gash on his thigh drenched his pants in blood, and Garsea had sliced Rig's shirt nearly in two, revealing a cut across Rig's back. With his body now more bloody than not, Tavi feared Rig could take no more.

Panting, Garsea said, "I'll give you this, whelp. You can take a beating. By Sicara's bloody teats, it is indeed a shame to waste your talent. But come, brother, meet the Sister with grace."

He thrust again but stumbled as Rig swiftly danced away from Garsea's knife. In an instant too quick for Garsea to have seen, Rig glanced toward the doorway, seeking Tavi.

A look of relief washed over him when he spied her eyes, low and peering at the door's edge. *He feared I'd left him.* The idea cut, but she guessed it wasn't unwarranted given all he knew about how people within the Mājas operated. Her own house loved the mantra, 'Cut your losses,' and she knew it applied to people as well as deals or rotten cargo.

The expression of relief quickly faded, and he gave her a single nod. *He's signaling he's ready for me.* Tavi's insides seized with panic. She'd talked a big game but feared she couldn't deliver.

Octavia thought of her father, who excelled at the game, and considered what he would say to her. *Focus, Octavia. Cleo, Rig, Gavino, and sweet Sabine have all done their part. Now it is your turn to prove yourself worthy of the Domanulos.*

Rig hadn't even tried to land a cut on Garsea but now thrust his blade toward the more experienced fighter. Garsea fended him off, but Rig had taken the offensive and maneuvered the fight closer to the doorway.

Still shy of his twenty-fifth birthday, Garsea was by no means an old man. But Rig was fast and had youthful energy on his side. He continued attacking Garsea with swift slices and thrusts of his blade. Rig didn't let up and forced Garsea to the doorway.

As he fended off Rig's assault, he nearly stumbled into Tavi but with his back to her. Unaware that she lurked in the passageway, the position exposed him.

It was now or never. With all her strength, Tavi thrust her blade into his side. Unsure if one deep cut would be enough to end the man, she quickly withdrew her blade and readied to attack him again.

By the time her knife was free of his flesh, Garsea had spun to see who had knifed him from behind. As soon as he'd turned toward her, Tavi held her dagger with both hands and thrust it into his heart where Rig had told her to aim.

His lips parted in an 'O,' and his eyes were wide with shock. Garsea tried to speak, but blood bubbled up from his throat.

The coppery scent of fresh blood assaulted her nostrils, and her hands were sticky with Garsea's warm blood. She should have felt even sicker than she did before. But the heady sensations broke the dam of her overwrought feelings of fear and worry for Rig, the other members of their Sigil Five crew, and for herself.

Untethered from her usual command of her emotions, Tavi thrust her blade again into Garsea, and again, and again. He reached for the doorway and put a bloody hand on her shoulder as he tried to remain upright.

Tavi didn't flinch away from his grip. Instead, she pulled him even closer. This time, she thrust the blade into the side of his neck, sure that this cut would be the last needed to topple the mighty Vandu Garsea of Fen Menir.

With blood pouring from the gash, he managed a last word. "Why?"

As he crumpled to the pale golden stone floor, Tavi felt no remorse for the life she'd just taken, or disgust at her violence. She leaned down and used the man's own tunic to clean his blood from her blade. She whispered the answer in his ear. "Because you stood in the way of that which I desire."

When she rose, Rig's expression was one of fear. Not of what he'd done, but of her.

He whispered a prayer to Sicara to receive his 'brother.' The words were part of Fen Menir's death cult and likely programmed into him since he was a child.

Tavi had no time to waste words on Garsea. "Sabine," she said.

Like a magical spell spoken by an Artifexa mage, the lone word snapped Rig from his stupor. In only a few seconds, Rig's studied mask of competence and control returned.

"We know not what we'll see when we enter his bedchamber. You've done your part, Tavi. Leave Batiste to me."

She wasn't sure why he felt the need to remind her that killing Batiste was his job, but in truth, bloodlust coursed through her. Previously sickened at the thought of taking another's life, the idea of ending Batiste now thrilled her rather than sickened. *Does he recognize the look of bloodlust shining in my eyes?*

Rignar cracked open the door to Batiste's bedchamber. A woman moaned, not in pleasure, but from pain.

Her heart racing, Tavi pressed against Rig, urging him to enter. Hunkered, Rig tip-toed into the dimly lit room.

Peering over Rig's shoulder, Tavi spied Batiste lounging on the edge of a massive four-poster bed. At first, Tavi took comfort in the fact that Batiste remained fully clothed.

Batiste trailed a finger down Sabine's side. Sabine lay on the bed, not tied or otherwise visibly bound, but her body rigid yet eyes open wide, frightened and darting.

He has poisoned her, Tavi thought. She was familiar with this poison, being a favorite of Batiste and others within Māja Babesta.

Distilled from the bark of a hestan tree, related to the bush that gave people the nys't painkiller. From hestan bark, skilled Artifexa alchemists create a slow-acting poison. The toxin first paralyzes the victim so that they are fully awake, but unable to move or escape. It could take days for the person to finally succumb to the poison and die. In the meantime, they are aware yet helpless.

Rig continued to press forward, entirely silent, a slithering shadow of death. Tavi tried to match his silence but made a heavy footfall.

The sound caught Batiste's attention, and he rose from the bed. "Garsea, at last. I was ready to begin without you."

Sabine again moaned, the only action the hestan poison would allow.

Rignar rose, then, to his full height, and towered over Tavi's boorish uncle. "Night's Sister was promised two souls this night, and one will be yours."

Chapter Nine

With the Vandu blade in Rig's hand, her uncle's life would soon wane. In mere moments, the Domanulos would be hers.

Such an end felt too lenient a punishment for Batiste's many crimes. Besides, she wanted the odious pustule of a man to know it was *she* who had plotted for his demise, and to know why.

"Stay your blade, Vandu," Tavi said.

Batiste's expression of awed surprise gave way to bemusement when he realized Tavi had accompanied her assassin.

Batiste clapped slowly. "Bravo, little Octavia. Breaching the walls and successfully entering my inner chamber. I'd written you off as most likely to follow Gavino's lead and lose yourself in a comfort den in the Shills. But making a move to enter the game? Surprising."

"Aren't you even curious why?"

"Oh, I know why," Batiste said. He held up his hand and wriggled the finger on which he wore the Domanulos. "Gavino was not as sly as he thought. Yes, I knew he was making a plan to steal my power. I assumed, though, he planned to take the ring for himself. Why would he help you, I wonder, rather than keep it for himself and ascend to the Cordomis?"

Sabine moaned again, though this time more loudly.

"We must hurry, Mistress Octavia," Rignar said. "Sabine needs the counter active, otherwise it will be too late."

Batiste smiled again. "Oh, and don't forget the next rotation of guards. They will sweep the halls soon, and no doubt find evidence of your misdeeds."

Her uncle should have feared for his life but appeared blithely unconcerned about the Vandu assassin poised to end him. Panic welled inside Tavi. *Why doesn't he fear for his life?*

Rig sensed it too. "Something isn't right," he whispered to her.

Batiste laughed and spat out his words with a sneer. "The arrogance of youth. You really thought you could go from sitting in the stands of the arena to being the star attraction in the battle of the ages? No, my sweet niece, it is *you* who will die by Sicara's blade this night."

He picked up a small bell from his bedside and rang it once. "Come, Ser Nicandar. Make haste and rid me of the interlopers. I'm missing out on valuable time with my—gift." He cast a glance down at helpless Sabine.

The wall on the far wall opened, revealing a hidden passage. An older man, with grey at his temples and an aquiline nose, stepped into the room.

Tavi did not know who the man was, but both Batiste and Rignar's mouths stood open in shock.

Batiste stuttered, "What… What is the meaning of this? Where is Ser Nicandar?"

Rignar finally found his words. "Ser Mordranis?" He bowed. "Master…"

"Night's Sister feeds well this night." Ser Mordranis pulled a cloth from his waist belt and made a show of wiping his bloody blade clean then stowing it in his scabbard. "Don't worry about our mutual friend Nicandar. Ser Mélantos, Master of Fen Menir, saw fit to oversee this affair himself, so it is Mélantos' blood Sicara feasts on tonight. Your soul, Batiste, fuels Nicandar's well deserved ascension." He tsked. "Nicandar mourns the loss of Garsea, of course, but when playing the Great Game, sacrifices must be made. Isn't that right, Octavia?"

Unfamiliar with the players in Fen Menir house, she wasn't sure exactly what Ser Mordranis implied. She managed a slow nod.

"Well, Timonay, do not keep Night's Sister waiting. You came to complete a task your Mistress bade you to do, yes? Do not keep your patron waiting."

Tavi had many questions, but no time to ask them. Rig spun and sliced cleanly across her uncle's neck.

Time seemed to stretch. Batiste's eyes wide, his words gurgled, he said only, "No." His entire body slumped, looking like a marionette whose strings had been cut. As he fell, blood gushed from the gaping wound in his neck.

Tavi had wanted to look him in the eye and tell him exactly why he was being cut down. He and likely the powerful men at Fen Menir assumed Tavi's motive was purely to usurp Batiste's power. And that was a powerful motivator.

But she had wanted to kill him long before her cousin Junia had suggested the Domanulos heist. The untold suffering this dying man had caused to so many people not only in the Mājas, but across all of Partha… Tavi wished it was Batiste who'd ingested the hestan poison. He deserved the slow, excruciating death he'd so often caused.

But his life waned all too quickly. Tavi said, "You deserve to receive back all the pain you caused, but I'll have to settle for this."

Batiste hadn't the strength to respond, and Tavi feared he was unaware even of what she'd said.

"Hurry," Ser Mordranis said. "Take the ring. Now!"

Rignar did as his master commanded. He wriggled the Domanulos off of Batiste's round finger while Mordranis knelt and put two fingers to Batiste's limp wrist.

"Poise it near her finger. Hurry, Timonay. As soon as Batiste draws his last breath, you must ensure the Domanulos meets its new master."

Tavi held out her hand, her fingers trembling. The Domanulos contained no gemstones or ornate filigree. It didn't sparkle or glisten. Instead, it looked like a barely worked bit of silver metal. On its face, the Domanulos bore the sigil of Māja Babesta, three intertwined snakes representing wealth, power, and wisdom. Now, as Rig poised the ring near her finger, the engraved snakes writhed as if aware of their disrupted world.

"Now!" Ser Mordranis shouted.

Without hesitation, Rig shoved the ring onto Tavi's finger. The three snakes wriggled, and the sigil glowed purple. Tavi swore she heard the ring hiss.

Icy cold ran through her veins, snaking from her finger into her arm, neck, and then down into her body. Tavi didn't breathe, and it seemed like her heart had stopped.

Her head spun, and blackness played at the edges of her vision. Through bleary eyes, she stared down at the Domanulos.

The sigil glowed even brighter now, but the snakes writhed less furiously. They slowly circled around each other as the glow faded. At last, the snakes ended their death dance and appeared intertwined as they had been, as if nothing had happened.

Tavi gasped, sucking in air. The icy feeling faded, and her vision returned to normal.

Within moments, her body resumed its normal state. She felt no different, and though the Domanulos hadn't killed her, she feared it hadn't transferred its power to her either.

"Make haste, Timonay. Cut her with your blade," Ser Mordranis said.

Rig shook his head. "No—"

"It is the only way to ensure that Batiste's power transferred. The Cordomis will test her this way. Do as your master commands," Mordranis said.

Tavi held out her arm and gave him a nod. "He's right. Do it."

Tears shone at the corners of Rig's eyes, and he grimaced. Rig took a deep breath and nicked her arm with the tip of his Vandu blade.

A stroke of crimson bloomed on her inner arm, just over the blue veins of her inner wrist. The cut wasn't deep and couldn't have caused her to bleed out. But the Vandu's poison was so virulent, a mere nick from its blade would be enough to kill her as quickly as Batiste had met his end. Only the power of the Domanulos could save her.

Silence swelled in the chamber as they waited. Tavi's wrist itched, and a tickle worked its way up her arm, but the sensation soon passed.

Within moments, Mordranis pronounced, "The Domanulos accepts her. Congratulations,

Mistress Octavia, soon to be the newest member of Babesta's Cordomis." He bowed to her, as did Rig.

She wanted to hug Rig, then take him back to her chambers where she could thank him properly. But she couldn't show affection for her vassal servant in front of Ser Mordranis, Rignar's true master. Besides, she had to do whatever she could to save Sabine.

Mordranis stepped over Batiste's now-still body, pushing Rig and Octavia out of the way. He pulled a small leather pouch from his waist pocket and forced Sabine's mouth open.

Her muscles were already becoming rigid, and he had to work to get her lips to part wide enough. Mordranis held an ampule of vibrant green liquid, shimmering in the dim light. He tipped the entire contents into the back of her throat, then forced her mouth closed.

Mordranis massaged Sabine's neck, forcing her body to take in the antidote to the hestan poison.

"Will she survive?" Tavi asked.

"She is no longer your concern," he said. Mordranis scooped her up and hoisted Sabine over his shoulder like a sack. "Come, Timonay, we must leave at once."

Tavi grabbed for Rignar's hand. "I will see you in a few days. Once things have calmed. I will keep my promise. You will be free."

Rignar's eyes held sadness like she'd never seen before. Like all the troubles of the entire world landed in those pale blue pools.

"What is it, dearest?" she asked. She should have taken care not to address him in such a familiar way, but the look of utter devastation on his face disarmed her.

Mordranis made his way to the hidden pathway he'd used to enter Batiste's chambers. "Say a quick good-bye, Timonay. We must make our way to Mara's cave. I think you're familiar with the location, no? A boat is waiting to ferry us to a ship in a secluded cove south of Partha."

Tavi clung to Rig's hand as he tried to pull away from her. "No. You can't leave. We succeeded." She raised her hand, showing the Domanulos, securely wrapped around her finger. "I am soon to be a member of the Cordomis, and I say he stays."

Mordranis, nearly to the hidden entrance, paused and turned toward her, Sabine still quiet over his shoulder. "Vandu Timonay performed two unsanctioned hits on Fen Menir brothers. Under the oldest and most sacred laws of our house, Ser Nicander has no choice but to order

Timonay's life forfeit. If he stays in Partha, he will be hunted by the brothers, his soul offered to our dear Mistress, Sicara."

"But I'm the one that killed Garsea. They should punish me instead."

"It was self-defense, Mistress. You are within bounds to yourself, even against a Vandu."

"Batiste was a prig, but he was second-in-line to succeed Fortunata. Surely Rig's crime against Batiste, which I now have the power to pardon, is worse than killing two guards, even if they are members of Fen Menir."

Mordranis gave her a wan smile. "You have much to learn, Mistress. You think you could have killed Batiste, even with your young assassin's help, if it had not been sanctioned?" He shook his head, his tone condescending. "Fen Menir has had a standing order to accept any requests for a hit on your dear uncle."

"Order from whom?" Tavi demanded.

"From the only one with the power to give such an order," Mordranis said.

He meant Fortunata.

Tavi's voice was a strained cry. "No. This cannot be. If it is riches Fen Menir desires, then they can have it. All that accedes to me, I will gift to your house. You and Ser Nicandar can split the fortune and be nearly as wealthy as Fortunata."

He gave her a tired, wry smile. "You cannot buy your way out of every misfortune, Mistress. And let that be your first lesson in this great game we play. As in Duple di Marc, the strategy game so loved by the Mājas, all moves come with a cost. Though this loss may feel unbearable to you now, in time you'll reflect and agree that it was, in fact, a worthy price to pay for ascension to a seat of power in the most powerful Māja in Partha."

Mordranis gave her a small nod and disappeared into the dark corridor of the hidden passage, taking Sabine with him.

Hot tears welled, and her body trembled as she pulled on Rig's arm. "No, you can't leave me. Not now. Do not abandon me in this odious house littered with bodies and stinking of death."

Tears stained his cheeks, and Rig sighed. "It was a beautiful dream, Tavi, and that's how I'll be to you now. A friendly specter keeping you company in the dark of night."

Rig pulled Tavi to him, his arms firm around her waist. Loss drained her reserves, and her legs felt weak beneath her. Rig held her up, and lent

Tavi strength she feared she didn't possess without him at her side.

Rig dipped his head and kissed her one last time. "Perhaps one day on a far shore, we'll meet again."

With her eyes still closed, Tavi savored the taste of him. Then Rig's warmth was suddenly gone. He swept from the room, gliding like smoke and disappearing into the dark.

In the days to come, Mistress Fortunata would reward Tavi for her daring play, Batiste's blood fueling her ascension to the inner circle of the most powerful house in Partha. The Cordomis would welcome her, and her grandmother Fortunata would silently approve of Octavia meting out justice. Justice Fortunata could not, as Batiste's mother, bring herself to deliver.

But now, the night's energy waned, and Octavia toppled to the floor. She landed in a heap beside her dead uncle, the turn of events denying her the opportunity to bask in the glory of their success with the other members of the Sigil Five.

When the guards arrived, as Batiste had promised they would, Tavi merely raised her hand in the air, brandishing the Domanulos.

They knew what it meant and immediately knelt in supplication.

The moment of her crowning brought no joy. She ascended alone. Her lover, protector, and only genuine friend was lost to her. Heartache was the price Octavia paid for power. A love she'd never forget, and a cost she'd never forgive.

"What have I done?" she asked herself.

A Message for Rhoji

Rhoji leaned against the white-plastered railing of Ser Chervais' villa. Warm sea breezes twirled his blue feather earring. Hiyadi, the Big Brother sun, kissed Bardivia's western shore, setting the sky ablaze.

He glanced up and eyed Niyadi, the Little Brother sun, still high in the sky. *That is me,* Rhoji thought. Destined to follow in his older brother's footsteps, yet carry the combined hopes of a people on his shoulders.

To escape the Dynasty's grasp, Rhoji, Eira, Mishny, Shel, and Imbica made their way to Bardivia, while Quen and Aldewin took a different path. Once Ser Chervais, the Bardivian wine merchant he'd met in Qülla, learned that Rhoji was Santu's son, he'd promised Rhoji work and a place to stay if he came to Bardivia.

The inducement had taken Rhoji by surprise. *Ser Chervais didn't even know me.* But once in Bardivia, it didn't take long to understand why Ser Chervais and other nobles had a growing distaste for the Dynasty, and why they were desperate for a 'savior.'

The Dynasty's encroachment on Bardivia's sovereignty had begun in earnest during Xa'Vatra's father's reign. When Santu, Rhoji and Quen's father, had abdicated his role as Consular, the Dynasty filled it with their own pick. Now Nóito, a Dynasty faithful, occupied the Doma di Consular, home of Bardivia's ruling family.

While Nóito had been the Dynasty's puppet, Xa'Vatra accelerated the effort to eliminate Bardivia's independence by installing a cadre of Kovatha mages to hassle the locals into submission. Bardivians resented the idea that they required policing by the capital's enforcers of not only Dynasty law, but Xa'Vatra's erratic missives mandated by her whims.

Rhoji, who looked so like his father, reminded Ser Chervais of better times. Of the prosperous era when Santu had been Consular. The times before the Little Brother sun began his journey to Vay'Nada, bringing the once-every-three generations dark nights, and of the times before dragons roamed their skies.

That is why Ser Chervais is eager to assist me. He and the other merchant leaders wish for me to replace Nóito, the Dynasty's puppet.

True to the promise he'd made in the capital, Ser Chervais set Rhoji and the pod up in his older villa high atop Orju Crest, the high hill in Bardivia that houses the nobility district. Rhoji glanced up at Orju Crest now and spied Doma di Consular, the estate owned by Bardivia but lived in by the city-state's Consular.

I lived there. So long ago.

Rhoji recalled spring and sitting beneath a blooming plum tree. Soft petals drifted on gentle sea breezes and fell to the grass, creating a pale pink carpet. Suliam, his mother, read *The Prince and the Peacock,* her voice soft but clear. He and Liodhan had played a game of chase, and Rhoji pretended to be disinterested in the story.

I'd hung on her every word.

To quell the pain of losing her, Rhoji had tucked memories of his mother deep inside. Now though, in Bardivia, the salty sea breezes and plum blossoms wrested the recollections from the dark place he'd stowed them. Bardivia felt more like home to him than the Sulmére ever had, and it made him yearn for his family.

But two of them live no more, and I'm uncertain of my sister's whereabouts. Are Liodhan and I now all that remains of Santu and Suliam's legacy?

Behind him, Eira pushed aside the gauzy curtain and handed Rhoji a cup of Bardivian gold. "Courtesy of Ser Chervais," he said. Eira sipped the wine as he hooked an arm around Rhoji's waist. With his eyes closed, Eira breathed in the sea air and smiled. "Did anyone ever have a more pleasant house arrest?"

Rhoji gladly took the wine. "We're not under arrest." The wine's tangy sweetness was like nectar of the gods after the dank water and homemade spirits they'd suffered for months on the road.

Eira wiped a drop of wine from Rhoji's lip and laughed. "Maybe not technically. What would you call it?"

He thought about the matter for a moment. "I prefer to think that we're choosing Ser Chervais' hospitality rather than being hauled back to Qülla by Dynasty Kovathas." He sipped the wine and gave Eira a wry smile. "Okay. Sounds like house arrest, huh?"

Eira's gaze fixed on the pink-tinged sky and twinkling azure sea. He said, "What I don't understand is why *not* arrest you? I mean, Xa'Vatra clearly knows that the Bardivian guilds want you to replace their lackey, Nóito. I hate to speak it aloud. But Xa'Vatra could just order—"

"To have me killed? Yes, that she could do. All too easily." Even the quality wine and incredible view couldn't prevent his mood from dampening upon thinking of how precarious his situation—his very life—was.

Eira caught Rhoji's gaze. "Why the elaborate game of cat and mouse? Does she just enjoy toying with her prey like an overly indulged house cat?"

"Oh, I'm sure Xa'Vatra enjoys the game. But no, I don't think she keeps me alive simply as a jape. Sers Chervais and Modishan say she's afraid to end me," Rhoji said.

Eira laughed again, his voice melodious and clear. "Xa'Vatra? Afraid? Now *that* is a jest."

Rhoji gave a wry chuckle, but his mirth soon disappeared. "Xa'Vatra may have more to fear than anyone else in the realm. What is that Vas O'Nai saying? 'To conquer one's fears, own them.'"

Eira took Rhoji's wine cup. "Oh no, you're quoting that insufferable twat Vas O'Nai. Best take your Bardivian gold before you recite O'Nai's *Seven Sutras of the Golden Son*."

Proffering a fake pout, Rhoji held out his hand for the cup. "I promise. No more Vas O'Nai."

Eira gave him a sideways glance but gave the cup back. "So, you're saying she fears you therefore keeps you in a cage like she does with powerful creatures in her Menagerie."

Like Xa'Vatra did to Quen. But Rhoji didn't speak that thought aloud. Instead, he said, "I think Chervais and Modishan have the right of it. Santu was beloved by the people of Bardivia. Their last great Consular before Xa'Vatra filled the vacuum of his esteemed presence with a limp carrot of a man."

"Ser Chervais said Xa'Vatra's hand is so far up Nóito's ass, 'You can see her fingers coming out of his throat when he talks.' His words, not mine."

They both laughed. Rhoji said, "Yes, well, Bardivia's Master Merchant's Guild loathe Nóito. They know nothing of me. But since I, apparently, look like my father did in his youth, they're willing to raise me up to Consular and depose Nóito. With their fervor for rebellion frothing, Xa'Vatra must know that if she committed violence against me, it would create all-out war with the guilds."

The pregnant silence of their heavy thoughts filled the space between them. Eira refilled their cups as they watched the sky fade from bright pink to dusky violet.

Though Ser Chervais' villa wasn't as opulent as many on Peacock Hill, the home came with a well-stocked wine cellar and a security force.

The bellicose wine merchant didn't provide for Rhoji and the pod simply out of the kindness of his heart. Though Ser Chervais was certainly kind, he was also a politically astute operative at the center of the two-decades-old desire for Bardivian rebellion against the ever-encroaching Dynasty. Ser Chervais and the Guild Lords were bribing Rhoji, plain and simple. Doing their best to induce him to become the thing the Bardivian Merchant Guild Lords desperately desired. *The one who will lead their rebellion against the Kovan Dynasty. Against Xa'Vatra.*

Though Rhoji had wished to become Bardivia's Consular since he was old enough to form a desire, he hadn't planned on earning the title by becoming the face of a rebellion. With each passing day, the collective hopes of Bardivia's people added to the weight he carried on his shoulders. Weight that included a gnawing concern for the wellbeing of his sister. *Quen, dear sister, I shouldn't have abandoned you into Aldewin's care. If I cannot properly fulfill my duties as first kin, how can I be master of an entire city?*

Eira, though, was a salve to Rhoji's aching heart. He kissed Eira, tasting the golden wine on his lips. "You are the only reason I don't go mad like a caged animal."

"That's because I know how to give you proper indoor exercise." Eira wrapped his other arm around Rhoji and undid his shirt laces. "Let us go inside," he whispered and playfully nibbled Rhoji's ear.

The heat rising between them intoxicated. Desire swept both boredom and worry from Rhoji's mind. One hand undoing the laces of Eira's shirt, the other pulling him closer. Rhoji kissed him deeply. His voice husky, he said, "Liberate me from this cage."

Eira took Rhoji's hand and led him to their bedroom. Before they crossed the threshold, a soggy breeze tickled Rhoji's ear. Someone whispered his name.

"Rhoji…"

He brushed stray hair from his face and rubbed his ear. Rhoji released Eira's hand and peered over the balcony rail.

"What is it, sol'dishi?" Eira asked.

Rhoji saw no one in the bushes on the hillside below. "I thought… Did you hear someone call my name?"

Eira shook his head.

Confinement is turning my mind to curdled drey's milk. He was about to turn and follow Eira inside, but a glistening flash caught his eye. Only a few feet away, a fine mist coalesced into a small, swirling ball of water. At first, it was only the size of a fist but grew as it gathered moisture. Within a few moments, the swirling water ball was the size of a person's head.

Rhoji called over his shoulder, "Do you see this too?" *Please tell me you see it and that I'm not going mad.*

Eira's mouth agape, he said, "Yes, but what is—"

From the swirling water, a gurgling voice spoke. "Rhoji, I have news about Quen."

"Is that… Aldewin?" Eira asked.

The water answered. "This is Aldewin. With the help of an Enar'atori aboard the ship *Sicara's Bane,* I will tell the tale of what befell Quen and I after we parted ways."

Rhoji and Eira were rapt, eagerly expecting more. The tightly wound mass of water dissipated. The mist spread and soon evaporated back into the coastal air.

"Wait—dammit, what happened?" Eira asked.

Rhoji's heart thundered, his palms clammy. *"Befell Quen…" I don't like the sound of that.*

As quickly as the watery sphere disappeared, another formed. Again, Aldewin's voice warbled from the spinning water.

"Quen and I never made it to Val'Enara. Archon Kine, in the guise of Val'Enara's spirit guardian, Hooxaura, blocked…"

Here, the message was unclear and faded. As before, the twirling mass became misty vapor, then disappeared entirely.

"This message does not allay my fears." Rhoji wiped his sweat-soaked brow.

Eira shook his head. "Wait. Perhaps there is more. We don't know—"

A new coalescence of vapors appeared. The beginning of this message, lost somewhere in Juka's breeze. "... discovered she was Nixan. Suliam, duped by Nevara, member of a dragon cult... Sol'iberi... Volenex."

Rhoji and Eira pressed forward. The swirling harbinger transfixed their gaze until, like the others, it disappeared.

Rhoji ran a hand through his hair and nearly tore out a chunk. "What for the love of the Three is he talking about? These words arrive half-formed. Suliam duped?" His laugh was bitter. "My Madi was not the sort to be played."

Eira pressed Rhoji's hand in his. "But Nixan? Did you know?"

Before Rhoji could answer Eira's question, another wet message arrived and then another until they'd listened to nearly a dozen. Each successive dispatch appeared more truncated than the last. By the end, Rhoji and Eira stood in Niyadi's pale light, staring at the horizon in silence.

Rhoji hadn't cried since the day they'd found Pahpi's charred remains, but tears stained his cheeks now. "A dragon?" The question was wholly inadequate to cover the situation, but it was all he could manage.

Eira released Rhoji's hand and fell backward onto a chair. His face was pale, and tears welled in his eyes. "How?" He stared up at Rhoji, wiped a tear, and asked, "Did you know? That she was Nixan? That she was—a beast inside?"

Instinct told him to lie. If being Nixan is enough to get a person put to death, someone harboring a known changeling often fared no better.

As if reading his thoughts, Eira said, "If we are to love one another, we cannot harbor secrets. Tell me the truth, Rhoji. Did you know?"

Rhoji sipped the wine and let out a long breath. "Yes."

There is it. Simple. To the point. And likely the end of what could have been.

"I see." Eira drained his cup. He stood and said, "I need time alone—to think on this."

Rhoji grabbed his arm. "Think on what? That I protected a person I love from being hunted like an animal and slaughtered by a fearful mob?"

When he turned, Eira's eyes were red-rimmed. "While you protected your sister, you put my sister and the rest of us in danger. Did you ever think of that?" He gently pulled his arm away and left Rhoji standing in the now-chilly, early eventide breeze.

By the time he drained the wine cup, anger displaced sadness. Frustrated, he tossed the metal wine cup as far as he could throw as he uttered a primal scream. It was loud enough to rouse the household and would likely bring the two mercenary guards Ser Chervais had sent to protect him. *Let them come. What shall I tell them? That my dear sister is Vay'Nada spawn? That will take the weight of their expectations off my shoulders.*

He wanted to be angry with Quen. For taking his Madi from him. For being the root of all his troubles. And somehow—he didn't yet understand the connection—he felt certain that Quen was the reason their father died, too.

I should hate her. By the gods, Quen is like an embodiment of Vay'Nada, casting a shadow over all I do.

But try as he might over the years to truly despise his sister—and he had tried his best—Rhoji couldn't hate her. Quen hadn't asked to be born cursed as she was. And he'd known her human half. *Quen—our Quen—is not a daughter of the Shadow.*

"By the gods, my anger lies within," he said aloud. "Eira, you were right. I didn't fully consider you, or Shel, or anyone else." *And how can I be a father to all Bardivia, when I cannot even look out for you, Eira?*

Someone pounded on the door to his bedroom chamber but didn't wait for an answer. Mishny barged in. Her voice was loud and angry. She demanded, "What did you do to Eira?"

With his back to her, Rhoji wiped the tears of sadness, frustration, and anger from his face. He wished now he hadn't thrown his cup like a fool because it would have calmed him to drink more of Ser Chervais' wine. Rhoji turned and said, "I did nothing to him."

Mishny plopped down on the chair where Eira had been sitting and put her boot-clad feet on the balcony rail, her legs crossed. "Look, your little lover's spats are the only entertainment we've got in this glorified prison. But for the love of Lumine's teats, unless you want the Dynasty to send a Kovatha warden to watch our every move, you gotta learn to control that temper."

"I don't need a lecture from you, Mishny."

"Well, you need one from somebody and I'm the only one here." The fire in her bright green eyes matched the intensity of his.

"I got a message. A bad one. And Eira heard it and he's—upset. We both are," Rhoji said.

Mishny glanced around, searching for the elusive messenger. "We had no messengers today. What are ya talking about?"

"It was a message from Aldewin, delivered by an Enar'atori."

Mishny's brow furrowed. "An Enar-a-what?"

"Sea Singers. They ask the waters to carry messages long distances. Clever magic."

Her eyes narrowed, and her lips pulled tight. "Damned Aldewin. What did the Northman say?" Then, as though a dark thought dawned, she asked, "Did he do something to Quen?"

Rhoji gave a wry laugh. "I thought you hated Quen. What should you care if Aldewin harmed her?"

As if his words were salt in an open wound, she rose and, hands on hips, said, "*I* don't care what happens to her. But *you* do." Her voice rose, and hot tears sprang to her eyes. "We're a pod now, and you shite-eating lot is all I have left, see? So, if that Northman, who I didn't trust from minute one, did something to your blood-kin— By the Three, I will put a blade through his foul heart." As if to punctuate the passion of her vow, she pulled the dagger from her waist belt.

Rhoji gently pushed her dagger hand down and donned a weak smile. "Aldewin didn't kill or harm Quen." *I hope she doesn't thrust that blade through my foolish heart when she hears what happened to Quen—and the truth I hid all this time.*

A tsunami of thoughts crashed onto his mind's shore, carrying a vision of machinations previously hidden. As Mishny waited for answers, realizations put puzzle pieces together. Like a game of Duple di Marc, Rhoji saw all the cards laid on the table, and understood finally why Xa'Vatra had issued the bizarre edict that singled out his sister with the bi-colored eyes.

Only seconds before, he'd wanted Mishny to stow her blade. Now he was ready to ask her to wield it. Not to hunt down Aldewin, and certainly not to harm him or anyone in their pod. But to ready herself for battle against their true enemy.

"Come, Mishny. Let us find Eira and send for our messenger. We must speak with Ser Chervais at once. There is more to Xa'Vatra's plan than we previously knew. And I fear that we have sent Shel and Imbica into more danger than they know."

For a Consular's Wife

To ensure the realm prospers,
        Honor the gods in all things.
Mirror the Trinity,
        By two, then one.
Sons come first,
        As Hiyadi and Niyadi once did.
Bold and blazoning,
        Pillars of strength for the people.
A daughter follows,
        Pale and wan.
Shining Lumine's glorious light,
        By day and by night.
Secure the Trinity on Menauld
        For Vindaô's prosperity.

Dear Consular's Wife,
        Your duty is clear.
Produce a Trinity for Bardivia,
        To have your Consular's ear.
Birth the Three to secure the realm,
        And continued reign of your king.
Complete the circle, and people will rejoice,
        Forever your name they will sing.

—From *Annals of the Consular*, First Era,
Bardivian Archives

SULIAM'S SECRET

Suliam

Niyadi's midday light warmed her skin as Suliam whispered the poem again. "And forever your name, they will sing."

She stared at the turquoise waters of Doj'Enara Bay, sunlight twinkling like diamonds on the gentle waves. Warm sea breezes ruffled the silk curtains of her private patio overlooking the sea. Tendrils of her black hair blew free of her elaborate braids.

Representative of Niyadi's grace, her second son called from the garden below. "Madi, look at me," Rhoji said. Under the watchful eye of his governess, Rhoji twirled as he tried his best to follow the steps of the Vindaô Winefest dance.

Suliam clapped. "How graceful," she called. And he was—for a four-year-old boy.

Here, in the rarefied air of the palace, on the highest land in Bardivia, Suliam's life was nearly perfect. Their arranged union forged alliances but blossomed into mutual admiration and eventually deep love. When Santu secured the seat of Consular, Suliam and a trio of mid-wives secured his claim with the birth of Liodhan.

Suliam had completed the first and most important task for a Consular's wife. She'd given birth to a firstborn son. To the Bardivians and the people across the Vindaô Province over which her husband ruled, Liodhan would embody the strength of Hiyadi, the most cherished god of the trio of deities, blessing their sky.

Two years later, sweet Rhoji followed. Bardivians toasted Suliam for honoring the Trinity by birthing two sons. The Vindaô people enjoyed a period of peace and contentment.

Suliam craned and raised her hand to shield her eyes from the bright light of the twin suns. She peered north, beyond the edge of the bay. The far hills should have been vibrant green this time of year, covered in flourishing vines growing the region's precious purple cargo.

Yet this year, the hill appeared dusky and brown. Juka's breath did not blow wet breezes over the Vindaô's land. Drought plagued the vineyards and farms. Grapes had withered on the vines. Even the olive presses remained quiet.

"They will blame me for this," she said aloud.

Deep in her thoughts, she hadn't heard Santu's soft steps enter from behind. He wrapped firm arms around her waist and planted a feathery kiss on her neck. "Who will blame you for what, sol'dishi?" His whiskers tickled, and heat bloomed on her neck.

"'Mirror the Trinity, by two then one.' I have failed you, and the land suffers because of it," she said.

Santu spun her to face him and wiped a tear from her eye. "Do not worry yourself so, sweet dove. It is a drought, not the gods or fate. And certainly not your fault."

Suliam's brow crinkled. "Don't make light of this, Santu. You believe in the gods, don't you?"

He pulled her close once again and planted a soft kiss on her pouty lips. "I studied at Val'Enara and honor the gods. You know this. But old Vindaô superstitions aren't in the holy writs taught at the Pillars. Gods and spirits have more important matters to concern themselves with than whether we have a child."

His words didn't comfort Suliam. She was born in Partha and not Bardivian by blood, but she took her binding oaths to heart. Her vows bound her not only to Santu, but to Bardivia and the Vindaô Province.

Suliam pulled away from Santu. His disregard of her fear raised her ire. "How can you dishonor me this way?"

Eyes wide and his mouth open in shock, he tugged at her hand to pull her back. "Apologies, sol'dishi. I only meant to comfort you, not offend."

Santu gently pulled, and Suliam swayed back into his arms. Lips to her ear, Santu whispered, "If it will ease your mind, we could try." His lips meeting hers, Santu's warm hand covered her breast while he pulled her into him.

Suliam's anger melted as his lips bent to her breast. She whispered a prayer to Night's Sister, the moon goddess. "Lumine, grant your blessing. Grace our union with your light."

She then tugged off Santu's belt as she kissed him deeply. Suliam unraveled her braids and welcomed her husband to her bed.

• • •

Summer passed without a single drop of life-giving rain. Suliam's womb remained as barren as the vines.

Though Santu placed no blame on her head, the people of Bardivia did. At first, they merely grumbled quietly into their cups. Some voiced sympathy for Suliam and made offerings at Lumine's shrine. Pale white flowers covered the ground of the temple and bolstered Suliam.

But that autumn's harvest was the worst in two generations. Purses were nearly empty, and children's bellies rumbled with hunger. People raised sour voices against their Consular's wife.

Santu ignored their grumbling. *Easy for him,* Suliam thought. After all, it wasn't Santu they impugned.

Desperate for her family to continue to hold their place of honor, Suliam consulted midwives and healers from near and far.

She tried every remedy, tincture, and poultice they offered. Counting the days between bleeds with meticulous precision, she coupled with Santu only when the lead midwife told her and never in between.

After several months, Santu grew grumpy at being denied spontaneous lovemaking with his wife. "I want to make love to you, Suliam. Not perform like a trained dog when commanded."

Santu did not answer her call the following day or the next. He said he had urgent business to attend. Suliam worried that in her effort to honor the Trinity, she'd lost her husband's affection.

The great wheel turned. The new year came with dark whispers. It was the first year of the Long Dark. Wee Niyadi had begun his return to the dark realm. Niyadi's pale light no longer banished the dark. Bardivia once again knew total darkness, if only for a few moments nightly.

Panic swelled, and people even called for Santu to step down.

"I cannot control the weather," he bellowed. Santu had long denied that magic could heal the land. But to appease the people, Santu implored Doka Pillar's Archon to bless the vines. "If magic can make the farms flourish, the Archon of Doka will know how."

Archon Séchen traveled from one end of the Vindaô Province to the other, blessing roots, furrows, trees, and vines. Despite his entreaties to Enara's patron goddess, Lumine, rain didn't fall, and farms lay fallow.

Nine days past the return of the Long Dark, a new Bruxia entered the Doma and sought an audience with Suliam. Her house woman nearly turned the new Bruxia away, but Suliam halted her.

"Show the woman to my solar. I would hear what she has to say."

The Bruxia entered, her dark hair long and smooth. A thin hand emerged from a dark cloak. "I am Nevara," the woman said.

Nevara dipped in a curtsy, her head down in supplication. She glanced up at Suliam with eyes as dark as a raven's feather.

Suliam took Nevara's cool hand in hers, gave it a brief shake, and then let go. Something about Nevara made her heart race in a manner most unusual. *Is this excitement—or fear?* Suliam wondered.

"Whence do you arrive, Bruxia Nevara?" Suliam showed her a seat and called for the service of jessamine blossom tea.

Nevara took a seat, her eyes never leaving Suliam. Nevara avoided the question. "All the realm knows of your delicate problem, madame. And I am a Bruxia of immense experience, you see. I came as quickly as I could. To offer my services."

Suliam sipped her tea, aiming to appear nonchalant. Inside, her heart drummed faster and sweat gathered in her armpits. *Did the gods send this woman in answer to my prayers?* "What type of services, exactly?"

Nevara reached inside her cloak, and she produced a small vial. The silver liquid swirled, glistening in the afternoon light. "A special tincture of my design." She held it up for Suliam to behold. "Lumine's blessings in a bottle."

Nevara eyed Suliam, her gaze intense. "Follow my instructions, and with the aid of this potion, your womb will welcome the daughter you've prayed for."

Suliam reached for the bottle, but Nevara stuffed it into her cloak.

"Oh, I see. There's a catch," Suliam said.

Nevara's eyes twinkled, and she sat forward in her chair. "All magic comes at a price, don't you agree?"

Magical rules were not Suliam's forte, but she knew Vindaô law nearly as well as Santu's legal counselors. Born into Māja Babesta, the most powerful House in Partha, mentors had trained Suliam to command the respect befitting the most powerful house in Partha.

Mustering her well-practiced air of authority, Suliam said, "If you are a citizen of the Vindaô, I could command you to give me that potion."

Nevara chuckled and reached for her tea. "Who said I called the Vindaô Province my home?" Nonplussed and unbothered, she sipped her tea. "Shall I tell you the price I demand in exchange for ensuring the continued prosperity of this realm?"

Curiosity pushed her ire aside. Suliam nodded. "Please tell me then. For your guarantee of a daughter, what price?"

Smoothing her black hair, Nevara reached again within her cloak. This time, she produced a parchment. She removed the ribbon and unfurled the document before handing it to Suliam for reading.

> "By the tincture proffered, you will conceive Lumine's daughter, completing the Three. In exchange for this bountiful gift, said child will be Dragonborn and promised to the Dragos Sol'iberi."

Suliam paused in her reading and laughed. "Dragonborn?" She tsked and nearly dropped the scroll.

A dark cloud of anger descended on Nevara's once-still countenance. She held the bottle of swirling liquid like silvery mist in the air. "Mock me not, or this tincture will leave with me."

Suliam had taken many tinctures, medicines, and teas over the years. Most were brown or green and tasted bitter. But Suliam had seen nothing like the elixir Nevara held. Suliam could swear the waters moved of their own accord.

Drawn to the promise like the tide to shore, Suliam dropped the smirk from her face. She continued reading the scroll.

> "Upon the Dragonborn's first Promena, she must venture to Volenex. There, the Rajani of the Dragos Sol'iberi will welcome the Dragonborn with open arms

and lovingly attend her metamorphosis with gratitude for her vessel. Praise to Primal Dragos Madi. We praise the dragon reborn. Praise for the rebirth of our god, the Winter Dragon."

All the warmth drained from Suliam's face. Her head buzzed, and her sight blurred and narrowed as if gazing through a dark tunnel. Suliam experienced a waking vision.

A young woman stood on a dais. She resembled Suliam so precisely that, at first, Suliam believed she saw herself in the vision. Her memorable eyes displayed contrasting colors: one gold, the other an unnaturally vibrant blue.

Suliam saw the odd-eyed woman sway and weep. A long dragon snout erupted from the woman's neck and quashed the woman's guttural cry.

Suliam screamed and dropped the scroll. Her voice was hoarse, and she said, "What vile magic—is this the future I see?"

With a rapid and unnatural movement, Nevara snatched the paper before it touched the ground. "Sip your tea, Suliam," she commanded. Perhaps to mollify Suliam, Nevara added, "Grasping at the threads of the future is like hunting a greased eel. Worry not over visions, for our wants and fears influence our interpretation of them."

Still rattled by what she'd seen in her mind's eye, Suliam absent-mindedly sipped her tea. Jessamine blossom's sweetness lingers only as long as the water remains warm. Now cold, the tea had gone bitter.

Thoughts raced, and her stomach roiled. Suliam pulled a linen handkerchief from the sleeve of her tunic and dabbed her forehead. Suliam could not promise a child born of her womb to be a sacrifice for zealots. *I cannot give birth to a child only to have her meet the end I saw in that horrific vision.*

Indrasian defeated the last dragon at the dawn of the First Era. Using her reason to gather strength, Suliam talked herself out of fear. *Besides, dragons were not gods, only beasts. And a dragon cult?* She glanced at Nevara.

The woman's beady, bird-like eyes stared back.

This woman is nattered. A dragon god? This cannot be real. Suliam's fingernails clinked against the side of the cup as she pondered. *But if Nevara asks for a pledge to a fictional god, perhaps her potion is only water and glittery rock dust.*

As if sensing Suliam's thoughts, Nevara put the tincture on the table with the parchment.

"You doubt the veracity of what I have said. I see it in your eyes."

Giving a nervous laugh, Suliam's back straightened, and she shook off her earlier fears. "You expect me, a woman educated in Māja Babesta in Partha, to believe in dragon gods? What is that place you mentioned? Volenex?" She tsked.

Nevara eyed her coolly. "You do not have to believe in our gods." She tilted her head and narrowed her eyes at Suliam.

"What do you have to lose? You will remain barren if you do not follow my advice and use my elixir. And if your gods do not favor your fields this season, the people of Bardivia will turn on you and Santu."

The reminder of what fate would befall them deflated Suliam's confidence.

"Or…" Nevara said.

"Or what?"

Nevara's gaze landed on the elixir. "Follow my exact instructions. If what I say is true, you will birth a daughter in ten moon's time. Then, even if the realm suffers, they cannot say it is the fault of Suliam of Partha."

Suliam considered what the woman had said. Even if the tincture, whatever its contents, helped her conceive a girl child, it did not mean that the birth would mean the rebirth of a dragon god. It was too ludicrous an idea to give weight.

Convincing herself that Nevara was a nattered zealot, Suliam gathered ink and quill and signed the document.

Nevara held out the bottle, but as Suliam grabbed for it, Nevara pulled it back. "Remember, you must do *exactly* as I say."

Suliam nodded.

"One stopper in warm water each night exactly as Niyadi sets."

"One stopper," Suliam repeated.

"On the thirteenth day, bed Santu at Niyadi's last light. Not a moment before or after."

Suliam held out her hand for the potion. "Thirteenth day. Got it."

Nevara still withheld the bottle. "Do not couple with him before or after that day. Do you understand?"

Suliam nodded.

"Beat him away, if you must. You cannot take his seed a moment before, or all will be for naught."

"He is angry with me anyhow. It will probably take me thirteen days to lure him back to my bed."

Nevara's forehead smoothed, and she nearly smiled. "Whatever his feelings, you must gain what Santu has to give. Ensure that it happens. Do what you must."

Suliam blushed but agreed. And at long last, Nevara placed the silvery potion in Suliam's hand.

Nevara gathered the scroll and re-wrapped its ribbon, then stood and prepared to leave.

"Will you remain? In Bardivia, I mean. To see if your potion confers the boon you promise?"

Nevara gave her a slight nod. "I will attend the birth," she said.

Suliam shuddered. She didn't relish Nevara's dark presence at the birth.

She tucked the bottle of promise between her breasts and out of sight. "In ten moons, we shall see if you speak truth or lies."

• • •

Following the dark woman's instructions to the letter, Suliam's blood did not come for one moon cycle and then another. Though abiding by a strict clock for their lovemaking perturbed Santu, once Suliam announced she was with child, he was no longer cross with her.

For ten agonizing moons, the Tomo-Santu family and the realm impatiently waited. Spring arrived and proved to be as dry as the last. The curse, alas, had not abated.

But Suliam's swelling belly roused their last hope of appeasing their gods. The people stopped agitating sentiment to oust Santu as Consular.

The spring passed to summer as Suliam's waist widened. Pain wracked the Consular's wife on a hot summer evening as she played a game of Duple di Marc with Lio and Rhoji. "She's coming!" Suliam cried.

Suliam's housemaid whisked Suliam to her private chambers and called for the midwives. A governess shooed Lio and Rhoji away. Used to being at his mother's side, being abruptly shunted to the side caused Rhoji to call out in a pained cry, "Madi!"

Another ripping spasm wracked Suliam. She could do nothing to soothe her sweet boy.

"The pain is much worse this time," she sobbed.

Head midwife Liestra tried her best to console. "Girls pain their mothers more than boys, that is all."

Though meant to comfort, the words didn't ease Suliam's pain—or fears. The awful worry that she indeed carried an unnatural abomination in her belly had nagged away at her for ten moons.

No one had summoned her—how could they? No one knew. But as complete darkness descended, Nevara appeared.

Nevara glided across the room in her unnatural gait and soothed Suliam with a voice smooth as melted brie. "There, there, little dove. I am here. All will be well."

Nevara pushed Liestra aside and commanded her to mix a tincture from the herbs she'd pulled from her cloak. "Warm these herbs in water, then press the mixture into clean linens. Bring it to me—now, quick!" she commanded.

With deft hands and soothing words, Nevara coaxed the child from Suliam's womb. She cut the cord with pride and pronounced, "The girl child is born as promised."

She handed the crying babe to Liestra. Tears glistened in the corner of Nevara's eye, and she whispered a prayer only Suliam could hear.

"Hail to the Dragon," Nevara said under her breath. "Welcome Winter Dragon. You are home at long last."

She should rejoice now, but Suliam's blood ran cold. In that instant, she knew the mistake she'd made.

Now washed and swaddled, the midwife handed the warm, bundled baby to Suliam. Born with a shock of dark black hair like her father's and the dark blue eyes all newborns possess, the babe readily took to Suliam's breast. The baby sucked thirstily, as if she'd been starving in the womb.

Cradling the child in one arm, Suliam ran her fingers along the baby's neck. Feeling a ridge along the babe's neck, Suliam's hands trembled. *The sign of a Nixan.* Her fears had been realized. *I can never love this abomination. Not as I love Lio and Rhoji.*

Staring down at the wee babe, Suliam's sorrow swelled. The child didn't choose their Nixan birth. Nor had she asked to be a vessel for a dragon cult's god. Her head swam as she recalled the vision she'd had over ten moons ago when Nevara had first darkened her door.

I cannot forgive myself for what I have done, and the Trinity will not absolve me either.

Tears streamed down Suliam's now gaunt and careworn face. She whispered an apology to the baby. A solemn expression of regret, which she meant with every fiber of her being. "I am sorry, Quen, for the burden I have placed on your life."

YLFA'S HEART

The frigid cold numbed her feet. "I can't feel my toes, mama," Ylfa cried.

Do I still have toes?

Ylfa blinked rapidly, trying to discern what was happening. The snowstorm obliterated the distinction between horizon and sky. Her entire world was a hazy white landscape scraped clean by blinding snow.

Ylfa rubbed her eyes. With panic in her voice, she cried, "Mama, I can't see you!"

Do I have eyes?

Burning cold gripped Ylfa from head to feet. Chills wracked her small body, and she shuddered.

Why mama not cradle me in her arms, wrap me in furs, and hum in my ear?

Quaking with bone-splitting cold, Ylfa prayed to Fréjoya, the patron spirit of winter's rain. "Please Blessed Sister of Ice, whisper my prayers into mama's ear. Guide her to me. I will die without warming fires to keep your chill winds at bay."

Does my mother still live?

Agony gripped her. Pain like a white-hot dagger shot through Ylfa like someone had split her open from neck to navel. She tried to scream—to call once more for her dear mother's arms.

Try as she might to call out, Ylfa heard no scream. If she had in fact cried, that sound existed, as did she, in a realm that was not reality at all. Or at least not as the people of Menauld know it.

Do I exist? I must, for I think the question.

Radiating tendrils of sky-fire surged through her, burning away every bit of Ylfa. Her blood, such as it was, consisted of blazing fire. And there—where her human heart used to be—a hollow. Vay'Nada's shadow crept, slinking into her cavernous chest.

The fire receded. Tight and constricted, her chest tingled. Something there, twisting, turning. Claiming.

More tendrils, but this time like vines rather than fire. Vines winding around the place where her heart used to be.

Ahead, a flash of indigo, like the color of a thick woolen shawl her mama wore around her shoulders. "Mama!" Ylfa cried.

But no one answered.

Silence. Stillness so whole it stifled.

Blinding white gave way to the dense dark of a moonless, starless night when even Niyadi, the Little Brother sun, slept. Snow blindness and numbing cold gave way to something far worse.

Emptiness.

Ylfa neither lay nor sat. Neither stood nor floated.

She was as ethereal as smoke and less substantial than a breeze. Ylfa was nothing, yet aware of everything.

Far off, as if across a windy expanse of blowing snow, someone called to her.

No, not to Ylfa. *Does the child still live?*

"Mama?" she called.

No, the voice was not her mother's.

It's a man.

Again, the quavering voice of an elder called to her.

She tried to speak. Her breath was as thin as a deceiver's promise. Ylfa opened her mouth and said out loud, "Mama."

A touch. Warmth at her side.

"Be still," he said.

Someone proclaimed, "She lives!"

A second man. Are there no Fyrstua sisters to welcome me home?

Tightness like massive talons pulled at her chest. Her skin was taut, like an animal hide curing on a wooden stretcher. When she blinked, her eyelids were like leaden weights filled with nettles.

Damp cold on her lips. *Water.* A trickle down her cheek. Ylfa tried to swallow the cool elixir of life, but her face didn't work properly.

Colors returned to her vision. She was not on the ice fields of the upper Vatnoyer—the Iska'kog lands. The place where she'd been born. Where she'd been the granddaughter of Thrud, the Crowskir of the mighty Spindel'vara Clan, the largest and most powerful in the upper Vatnoyer Province. *I left that place many years ago though, didn't I?*

Bleary shapes loomed over her. A bearded man bent with age.

She recognized him, but Ylfa should not have known him.

Ylfa is gone. She has been for years.

The woman blinked again, her focus returning. A second man, beside the first. A gold ring in his nose connected by a chain to a band on his ear.

I know him. He was a friend, she thought. Or a business confidante anyway.

"Where?" She coughed. "What…?"

Nearly lost to the Void, memories of her last moments returned. Of an altercation with a deceptively powerful young woman with one eye the color of a glacial pool, the other of bee honey. A giant snow tiger yowling.

Nivi. What did I do?

The young woman, hatred in her bi-colored eyes, moved as if in amber. Time slowed, but only for the attacker. The woman stabbed her in the chest with a very dull blade.

"The Doj'Anira… I failed my Exalted."

Prelate Vidar said, "Have no fear, Mistress of the Menagerie. The Exalted needs you still and offers a chance for redemption."

The other man held her hand and spoke excitedly. "Oh, my dear Pelagia, you are going to love this one." Anu'Bida sounded like a jubilant child salivating over a sweet roll.

Pelagia tried to push up, but immediately regretted it. Pain ripped through her chest, and she fell back. *Someone filled my chest with hot coals.*

"What in Vay'Nada did you do to me, Vidar?" Her voice was thick, and her words slow. Pelagia didn't look at her body, afraid of what she'd see.

Vidar pressed her back and placed a poultice on her chest. The compress stank of rotted seagrass, fish guts, and fermented beans. "What did I do? I did what I always do. Followed the commands of our Exalted."

Every breath brought a wave of nausea. Through gritted teeth, Pelagia asked, "And what did she command?"

"Like any great mother, our Exalted's commands are straightforward, and the consequences readily stated. And as you are aware, she will follow through. With the consequences of disobedience, I mean." Vidar brought a dropper to her lips to give her nys't.

Pelagia lifted a leaden arm and shoved his hand away. "No nys't yet. Not until I have answers. What did she order you to do, Vidar?"

"She commanded, 'Make her live, Vidar, or I will ensure that you die.' Quite a tricky thing, you see, as you had no heartbeat." He waved a bony hand in the air. "Oh yes, a moment exists between when the heart stops beating and the true end of life. Anyone well versed in the ways of Vaya di Soli knows this. But normally, it's up to the gods or Vay'Nada to reanimate the body.

And seeing as how I am neither god nor Shadow spawn, it seemed an impossible task."

Blackness played at the edges of Pelagia's vision. "I… died?"

"Quite," Vidar said.

A second attempt to rise went no better than the first. She wailed in pain.

Anu sniffed powder from a small turquoise-blue box. "Really, dearest. Rest. You are quite eager for someone who recently had a gaping hole in your chest where a heart should be."

Pelagia tried to feel her chest, but Vidar gently pushed her hand back to her side. "No touching until it has healed."

Vidar trickled cool water onto her lips, but her voice still rasped. "You—removed my heart?"

Prelate Vidar stroked his scraggly grey beard. "What else was I to do? Even for the best Val'Doka healers, your heart was quite beyond repair. No one could weave a healing bond for that damage. The Nixan girl did a number on it. Would have been better had she used a sharp blade rather than a glorified butter knife."

"If I have no heart—"

"Oh, but you do. Of course you do." He tittered. "Elsewise you wouldn't be talking to me, would you?"

Pelagia wasn't sure. *This entire conversation might exist only in my mind. Or perhaps I'm bedeviled by trickster spirits in the Void.* She felt so odd. Pelagia wasn't convinced that she was alive. *I am me, yet not.*

Pain drained her energy, but she wanted answers. Pelagia stared into Vidar's milky eyes and spoke with as much command as she could muster. "Vidar—*what* did you do to me?"

Vidar's eyes grew wide with excitement. "I performed a damned miracle, is what I did. I brought you back to life, Pelagia. But better than before I dare say." He nodded vigorously and beamed a smile of yellowed teeth. "Yes, yes. You'll see. Improved."

Anu'Bida gave a weak clap of his hands. "Oh yes. Better than ever." His voice dripped with sarcasm.

At least, that is what his tone sounded like to Pelagia. Everything felt—off.

But whether she was truly experiencing this conversation or living it only in a shadow realm, she was curious. "Better you say. How?"

"Your new heart is—unique. A moment of genius, I must say. Taken from a creature that is in some ways your better."

Pelagia's brows furrowed, and she was about to argue the point, but Vidar continued.

"Oh, don't pout. Just you wait. Your new heart, once you get used to it, will make you even more proficient at your job."

Anu'Bida put in, "You were already the best at what you did. Can you imagine what you'll be capable of now?"

Prelate Vidar said under his breath, "Gods help us if this goes too far."

Breathing made every inch of her ache, but Pelagia sucked in a deep breath, sighed and said, "Vidar, as Hiyadi is my witness. If you do not speak plainly and tell me exactly what you did, once I'm healed, I'll rip your chest open as you did mine. But I won't give you a shiny new heart. Oh no. I'll rip everything out of you that keeps your ancient hide alive. Bit by bloody bit. Slowly."

Anu laughed so hard he snorted. "She'll do it, Vidar." He slapped his silk-clad thigh. "I've seen her in her feral state. Vicious enough to make a seasoned soldier dirty his underclothes."

Vidar swallowed hard. "Simple, really. Wish I'd thought of it years ago. Well, sometimes a sword at your throat is all the motivation you need to perform miracles." He wiped his forehead with a sweat-stained cloth pulled from the sleeve of his robes. Tittering, Vidar said, "Of course without Yindrils, the whole thing is impossible. Gods welcome their souls."

Anu'Bida and Pelagia both said at once, "Vidar! What did you do?"

"To put a Yindril heart where your human heart used to be. It took much coaxing, but it finally fused with your body and now pumps your blood." Vidar returned the sweaty cloth back to his sleeve pocket. "Dear Pelagia, you now have the heart of one of Menauld's most magical creatures."

Like the sunrise on the longest day, understanding dawned. With a shaky hand, she gingerly touched her chest. "I have the heart of a—Yindril?" Memories flooded her mind. Of watching Kovathas with virtually no inherent ability to master Menaris become capable battle mages thanks to nearby Yindrils.

She remembered now. That had been her first gift to the Dynasty. Bestowing a Yindril on Xa'Vatra had gotten Pelagia the job of Mistress of the Menagerie and favored status with the Dynasty. With the help of her friend Anu'Bida of Māja Wix, Pelagia had helped Xa'Vatra acquire dozens of Yindrils to build her small but powerful Kovatha battle force.

Why did I never bother to ask why Xa'Vatra needed battle mages?

Because of their prized status, Xa'Vatra had issued an edict making it illegal and punishable by death to intentionally kill a Yindril. "Why would the Exalted allow you to sacrifice the life of a Yindril for me? Or does she not know what you did yet?"

"Oh, she knows. In fact, she authorized the action personally. Said, 'You can sacrifice up to three of the tree men Vidar. Just bring my Mistress back.'"

Anu'Bida nodded. "I was there. It's true."

"Anu, make your way to the Palace to give the Exalted the good news while I attend the Mistress. Xa'Vatra will hide her enthusiasm, mind, as she is loath to praise me. But she will be beyond pleased. This I know, for she has an incredibly important job for you."

"What job could be so important she'd risk three of her most prized possessions, worth more than their collective copious weight in gold?"

"A task you are uniquely suited for. And now—well, even more so."

Vidar bent closer. Gone was the excited expression of pride in his accomplishment. He set his jaw, and his lips were stern. "I only hope my miracle does not come too late."

"What task has the Exalted snatched my soul back from Vay'Nada's shores to do?

"You, Mistress, will retrieve the Heart of Menaris."

FEED THE ROOTS

Sølvi swayed on Jór's furry back as he carried her ever further into the Ghost Forest. With her arms outstretched wide, Sølvi's fingers swept low boughs. The crocodile bark was rough on her aged skin, now nearly as translucent as a dragonfly's wing. Twigs snapped as they passed, but otherwise the dense woodland was eerily quiet.

She and Jór had traveled far from the boggy coastal plains of the lower Myrskog. Sølvi had never ridden such a great distance. Towering pines formed a crowded canopy overhead, allowing little of the Brothers' light to penetrate.

Old Jór's labored breathing created steamy wisps like smoky dragon's breath. The narrow path wound up a steep slope. Tired from the morning's difficult trek, Jór struggled to clear the large tree trunks jutting across the trail. Roots twisted over and clutched boulders.

Sølvi patted Jór's side. "Not long now, old friend. Only a bit further and we'll rest for our midday meal."

Jór snorted. His foot clopped as it hit a sizable, winding root. They nearly tumbled, but Jór righted himself. The elderly horse carried his wizened companion upward toward their destination: the saddle of Widow's Rise.

Though the morning had begun chilly and spitting rain, Sølvi's resolve had warmed her. At the edge of her vision, the trees were like human silhouettes. Their branches like arms, their sinuous roots like legs spreading across the moss-carpeted woodland floor.

Sølvi hummed an ancient melody her mother had taught her long ago.

On the undulating waves of Mara's Sea,
We swim.
Over the tender roots of Skogi's Green,
We stroll.
Under the welcoming canopy of our forest abode,
We dance.

Hush…
Listen.

The Yindril's lament joins the cricket's lullaby.

Skogi's song soothes us—
We sleep.
Beneath sun-warmed skies, two-by-two,
We march.

Ever onward until we tire,
The Green hails us home.

Fear not the forest's dark, dear ones.
Skogi's roots await us all.

When they'd reached a clearing, Jór knelt. His legs trembled from the effort.

In her younger years, Sølvi dismounted without aid, bounding from her mount. Back when she'd ridden with the Jagaru in the Sea of Sands. When Sølvi had brandished a curved sword in one hand and a dagger in the other, she'd easily defeated two marauders at *once. Many decades ago. Before fleeing to the Myrskog to escape heartache.*

Now Sølvi's legs trembled as she struggled to dismount without falling. She grabbed the twisted branch she'd fashioned into a cane and eased off Jór's back.

After she dismounted, Jór fell over with a groan. Sølvi rubbed his soft nose.

"You are a kind pal, Jór, to help me do this." Tears gathered in her eyes. She bent and kissed his snout. "My only remaining friend."

The others were gone now. A lifetime of trials and triumphs. Of lovers won and lost. Children grown, families of their own, and now she'd lost them, too. This shredded her emotions the most.

Silent tears streamed as Sølvi unbuckled her pack.

"A sole duty remains," she said.

Jór had stopped in a wide clearing. White stones strewn across the ground shone in the dim light.

Sølvi retrieved a special treat for Jór from her saddlebag. She'd saved the honey oat cake for this moment.

"Enjoy, Jór. And make it last. This is all I have for you. "You'll have to forage on your way back to the village."

Despite her entreaty to eat slowly, Jór devoured his food in two bites. Sølvi chuckled as she nibbled the remaining rations. She'd saved her favorite bogrice, fish, and drey cheese steamed in giant tí leaves. Sølvi intended to savor the smoked fish's briny flavor and the cheese's slight funk.

As Sølvi approached a pile of rocks to sit, she realized the white blobs weren't stones.

"By Skogi's teats, these are skulls." She glanced around the glen, suddenly feeling as though eyes watched her.

Human remains littered the forest floor across the entire clearing. The already chilly day now felt colder. Sølvi wrapped her cloak tighter.

Sølvi remembered the song's refrain and sang it aloud to comfort herself. "Fear not the forest's dark."

The mossy wood, like an old friend moments before, now was like a surly hermit angered by her intrusion. Like a giant bellows, the Green sucked the fresh air from the glen, hoarding it for the shadowy spirits known as myrkandar. The Ghost Forest leeched what remained of her joy, pilfering it like a cutpurse.

Sølvi glanced at Jór. He lay where he'd tumbled over, his breathing steady. *Does he feel this bone-sapping cold as keenly as I do?*

She dug a woolen blanket from her bag and draped it over Jór. Her eyes darted. "This wood… Never have I felt frightened by the Green. I feel these woods watch us."

The old horse blinked slowly, and his eyelids drooped. Sølvi had planned to send Jór back down the slope after their meal. She didn't think it was fair to make him stay. He'd been too good a friend to suffer witness to her end.

But Jór was too tired to return. "My ritual must wait, then. Until Jór rests and has the strength to part these woods."

Sølvi drew her dagger from her bag and unsheathed it. The leather-wrapped hilt, once creamy white of a drey's skin, had darkened from her sweat and hand oils over the years. For years, she'd cleaned the blade and sharpened it daily though it was now dingy from disuse.

So much blood you have known, she thought to the blade. Sølvi flicked her thumb along the edge, and it sliced her onionskin-like flesh. *Still sharp, though.*

She sucked her thumb, the tangy taste of blood on her tongue. The flavor and odor awakened long tucked-away memories of combat she'd survived, and of the would-be attackers she'd defended against. She eyed the silver blade. *Even the blood of someone I thought I loved, but who took what wasn't his to take.*

Sølvi had come to the Ghost Forest in secret, and against the command of her clan's Leid and Eldurskir. She'd come to perform old magic—an ancient rite. From the days before Partha's Mājas. Rites from the age of dragons and legends.

In those days, so legend said, when the clan suffered famine or calamity, an elder's duty became a rite. Ancient, like wine to the vine, to protect the clan and gain the Green's favor.

"Back when the Green was thirstier, hey Jór?" Sølvi said. She chuckled, but Jór only snored.

It is not like Jór to sleep so soundly, but our journey was arduous. He just needs rest.

After finishing her meal, Sølvi ambled to a nearby tree and settled into its tangle of roots for a nap. The peaty ground was soft beneath her, like the comfort of a favorite chair.

Her eyelids heavy, Sølvi relaxed. *A quick sleep. Then I'll wake Jór and send him home. Before the wee sun sleeps. Before the myrkandar visit the forest.*

Sleep readily came to Sølvi. She slept a quiet, dreamless slumber.

A desperate whinny woke her.

Jór keened an unnatural throaty sound. Her eyes bleary, Sølvi wiped them to clear her sleep.

The Little Brother sun was nearly at his rest. *I slumbered too long.*

Jór flailed his front hooves as his back haunches sank into the ground.

"Jór!" she cried.

Sølvi used her cane to push up, but vines wound around her wrists. She pulled and writhed but more tendrils erupted from the soil, encircling her arms and legs.

Her voice was a strangled cry. "Jór! Get up. Pull yourself from the muck."

Sølvi yanked and wrestled as tears streamed down her cheeks. "Not my Jór. Take me, myrkandar. Release my sweet Jór. I came here to sacrifice myself, not him."

In answer to her plea, the Green sent a mighty wind that whistled through the pines high and shrill. The breeze sounded like a sorrowful song a weeping mother would sing for a lost child.

Jór's eyes showed their whites, and he snorted loudly. Slick sweat shone on his neck as he fought against the myrkandar spirits swirling around him.

"I beseech you, Jantu and all gods of the Green. Jór is not prepared." Her voice was raw and sounded like raspy reeds. "Take me," she sobbed. As she continued to struggle to free herself, heaving sobs wracked her body, and burning pain threaded through her limbs.

The shrill wind persisted, but now a second sound rumbled through the glen. A low hum, like the drums of the world itself, rattled through her. This new undertone felt like a song of hunger and longing, an eerie counterpoint to the high piercing screech of the sharp, sorrowful wind.

This thrumming grew more insistent and drowned out Jór's baleful cries. It vibrated deep in Sølvi's belly as roots sprang from the soil and ensnared Jór.

Sølvi tore at the thick roots encircling her wrists until her paper-thin skin bled. The forest's preternatural breeze swept her hair free from its tie. Her silvery hair now flew about her face.

Jór's remaining energy sapped, he could do nothing but pant as the ground swallowed him whole. Bound in place by twisted roots, Sølvi could only stare as her last best friend fed the ravenous Green.

Her throat raw from screaming, Sølvi's voice was a choked whisper. "It was supposed to be me."

Swirling leaves soon covered the spot where Jór succumbed. If she hadn't witnessed it, Sølvi would never have known Jór once lay there.

"Why?" she croaked.

A high-pitched whine was the Green's only reply.

Losing Jór drained the last of her strength. Sølvi gave up battling the roots and vines that held her fast. Once her struggle ended, Sølvi's labored breathing returned to normal. Her racing heart slowed and found a new rhythm that matched the thrum of the forest's hunger.

Once feared, Sølvi soon discovered that this beat was not unpleasant. The more she relaxed into it, the less melancholy she felt.

Sølvi had no way to measure time. She knew not how long she lay cradled in the roots. In time, she could not distinguish between her own gnarled hands and the finger-like roots tangling the forest floor.

At long last, Sølvi found her voice again. She sang, and her high, shrill tone matched the doleful, plaintive wind.

Sølvi had become part of the Green.

She *was* the Ghost Forest, and the woods were her.

Sølvi saw nothing yet witnessed everything.

One now with the Green, her roots spread like one enormous animal across the breadth of the forest. She fed the roots and became one with the silent wood.

• • •

For many seasons, Sølvi watched seeds sprout and elder trees fall. All fed the roots as Sølvi had. The song of the Green thrummed.

One day, Sølvi heard a new sound.

Always still, always listening, Sølvi felt the woman's footfalls before she entered the clearing. The woman's voice lilted above the inaudible hum of the Song of the Green.

"On the undulating waves of Mara's Sea, we swim," the woman trilled. Her voice was pitch-perfect.

"Over the tender shoots of Skogi's Green, we stroll." The woman whistled a few bars, and the mournful lullaby turned bright and cheery.

Nearer now, the woman's voice grew louder. "Under the welcoming canopy of our forest abode, we dance." She twirled as she said the word 'dance.'

She glimpsed something and bent. "What's this?"

The woman flicked golden leaves off a rotted pack. Her eyes darted around the glen, searching the sentinel trees as though they'd reveal the pack's owner.

The woman didn't realize, but the trees stared back.

Frayed by the years, the cloth disintegrated in the woman's hand. She flung the soggy remnants of Sølvi's pack to the ground and drew her cloak more tightly.

She stepped backward, and her heel caught on a skull fragment. As she glanced down, noticing now the stones were human remains, the woman gasped.

"Don't freak yourself out, Rin," she said aloud. Rin pulled a red scarf from her own pack and wrapped it about her throat for warmth.

Cold had descended on the once warm glen, and Rin's breath became a mist. Fog now crept along the forest floor.

Undaunted, Rin continued walking. She sang,

"Ever onward until we tire—"

Rin tripped over a large, twisted root shaped like an old woman's crooked arm. Densely packed leaves and moss absorbed the sound of her fall.

Rin tried to stand, but a branch snagged her cloak. She yanked free but tore her cloak further on the branch.

"You skishatur tree," she said. Rin kicked the branch that had tripped her. "My da made this cloak for me brand new for this trip."

Sølvi felt Rin's once joyful mood dissolve into a bubbling cauldron of fear and ire. *She did not come here to die as I once did.*

Rin's warmth suffused the deadly meadow. The rhythm of her pumping blood awakened the Green's hunger. Awakened *Sølvi's* thirst.

The Ghost Forest's rhythm thrummed louder.

Like the hand it had once been, Sølvi reached a gnarled root. She wrapped it around the woman's ankle, and Rin screamed. Trying to break free, Rin twisted her foot.

The roots circled more tightly. The Green made Sølvi more powerful than she'd been as a woman.

Rin's ankle bone snapped. She cried out and toppled to the ground.

Holding her ankle across her lap, Rin called out. "Help! Please— Anyone? Help me."

The Ghost Forest swallowed Rin's pleas like a ravenous man devours wild rice porridge.

The Green answered Rin's supplications with its shrill lament. Whistling through the pine needles, thundering in the roots beneath her.

"No," Rin whispered. Her voice was a croak. "I did not come here to die. I came to prove the legend untrue. You win, Skogi." She tried to chuckle, but it came out as a sob. "I believe. Free me, and I'll return to my people and tell them it's all true. I'll sing your praises, Skogi. Praise be to the Green." Rin bent low, touching her forehead to her knees.

Sølvi snaked a thin tendril to Rin's face and wiped her salty tears. She wrapped the horrified woman in her arms like she had long ago held her own newborn babe.

The forest pulsated with its song of hunger. Thunder rolled through the ground and into Rin. The forest's baleful tune danced on the breeze, and the chill froze Rin's tears on her face like glistening jewels. Sølvi's twisted roots encased Rin like a caterpillar in a cocoon.

Sølvi added her voice to the forest's song as Rin fed the roots. She embraced Rin in her gnarled limbs and sang the last words of the lullaby Rin had sung.

"Skogi's roots await us all."

Author's Notes

The Sigil Five

We learn much about Aldewin in *The Spring Dragon*, but there was an important relationship from his life in Partha that will become relevant to *The Summer Dragon*. To prepare for writing *The Summer Dragon* (Dragos Primeri 3), I needed to delve deeper into Aldewin's backstory to understand more about the events that led to him ending up in Indrasi.

I love a good heist tale and always enjoy crafting a story that puts together a group of characters who share a common goal. Aldewin's backstory gave me a great opportunity to fulfill my heist story dreams!

Writing *The Sigil Five* taught me much about Aldewin's past and lights the way for his future.

What do you think of Octavia, aka "Tavi"? While reading *The Spring Dragon*, did you suspect he had such a relationship in his past? Do you have speculations about how the events and outcomes of *The Sigil Five* will impact Aldewin in future stories?

SULIAM'S SECRET

If you've read *Season of the Dragon*, you know Quen's story began long before she was born. In the first chapter, we discover that her mother, Suliam, made a dark bargain with a shadowy woman named Nevara.

By the end of *Season of the Dragon*, we learn the details of Suliam's pact with Nevara, but the question endures: Why?

At last, *Suliam's Secret* reveals Suliam's motivations. Do you think she had a valid reason? Was she looking out for the people of Bardivia? Or for herself?

This story also shows readers a glimpse of Bardivia, a city we'll see more of in *The Summer Dragon*. Now that Suliam's essence has been subsumed into the reborn Quen, what impact will that have on our young heroine?

A MESSAGE FOR RHOJI

I wrote this brief scene while writing *The Spring Dragon*. I'd originally intended for *The Spring Dragon* to follow more viewpoints, with chapters from Rhoji's POV, and from other characters as well.

Ultimately, I chose instead to focus on Aldewin, Ishna, and Quen. Thus, this short Rhoji and Eira interlude was cut.

While reviewing things to prepare for writing *The Summer Dragon*, I came across this "lost" chapter, and thought readers might enjoy a glimpse of the life Rhoji and Eira are living during the action of *The Spring Dragon*. We'll definitely see more of Rhoji, Eira, and Mishny in *The Summer Dragon*.

In this scene, do you think Eira is being fair about what Rhoji did? Is he being overly harsh—or not mad enough? Would you have kept Quen's true nature secret from your lover and/or friends? How do you think this is going to impact Rhoji and Eira's relationship going forward?

Ylfa's Heart

As with the Rhoji and Eira story, I originally wrote this short as part of *The Spring Dragon* but cut it from the final book. I thought readers might enjoy seeing the moment when Pelagia revives after Vidar brings her back to life with a Yindril's heart.

I enjoyed discovering more about Pelagia and who she was before she became the Mistress of the Menagerie. Writing this scene gave me the idea of how Thrud and the Spindel'vara Clan were using dragon magic to fuel their thirst for power.

Seeing this glimpse of Pelagia, aka "Ylfa," does it change your view of her in any way?

FEED THE ROOTS

I wrote *Feed the Roots* before I penned *Season of the Dragon*. Originally, I wrote the story for a folk-horror anthology that didn't end up happening, so I hadn't set the story in the Dragos Primeri universe. Feeling the story had potential, I continued working on it over the years.

You might notice that the poem Sølvi recites in *Feed the Roots* appears in *The Spring Dragon*. The feel of the story fit well with the Vatnoyer region, and especially the Myrskog people. It was only natural, then, that I should revisit the entire story and re-work it to fit into the Dragos Primeri universe to include in this collection.

Though I've enjoyed *Feed the Roots* since I first wrote it, I love this final version! Reworking it into a folkloric story of the Myrskog people improved it.

If any story has my writer DNA wrapped up in it, *Feed the Roots* is probably it. This story has my heart!

Acknowledgements

A huge thank you to the Dragos Street Team! Y'all keep me motivated and fuel my writing more than you can know.

Thank you to Braken, cover artist for the Dragos Primeri series. Cover reveal day is always exciting, and I absolutely love this cover. Kudos!

I'm so excited I could work with Felix Farley, illustrator of this book. A versatile artist, I gave Felix free rein to create in whatever style he chose. I absolutely love the results and look forward to future collaborations with him.

Thank you to Vanessa Cesca for editing work and to Sarah from Behind the Pages PA for her continued support behind the scenes.

As always, thank you to Pete. He's not only my right hand at events but also a springboard for ideas and my beta reader. Cheers, sol'dishi.

And thank you, Dragos Primeri fans!

Natalie Wright

About the Author

Natalie Wright is a lifelong sci-fi and fantasy nerd living her author dream. She's likely ensconced in her dark academia den, penning the next story in her epic Dragos Primeri series. Natalie is the author of the multi-award winning novel *Season of the Dragon,* named a Top 10 Indie Epic Fantasy by Bookshop.org and Ingram. She's also the author the YA Sci-Fi series, H.A.L.F., and *Emily's House,* a YA paranormal fantasy novel with over 2 million reads on Wattpad.

When she's not writing, you'll find her playing fantasy RPGs, attending live theater, or binging shows on Netflix. Natalie lives in Arizona with her husband and two cat overlords and frequently visits her artist son in NYC.

You can order signed books, special editions, and book merch and view Natalie's appearance schedule at: www.NatalieWrightAuthor.com.

About The Illustrator

Felix Farley is an animator, illustrator, and fine artist working in multiple mediums. He is a graduate of Pratt Institute, where he studied 2D animation. Felix's capstone film, "It's Perfect," has been screened at the Alamo Drafthouse theater in Brooklyn as part of Pratt's Best of Show, and received an honorable mention in the East Village Film Festival. Felix lives and works in Brooklyn, New York.

You can view more of Felix's art at:
www.FelixFarleyArt.com
Instagram: @FelixFarleyArt

www.ingramcontent.com/pod-product-compliance
Lightning Source LLC
LaVergne TN
LVHW090516110826
845146LV00003B/875

* 9 7 9 8 9 9 2 1 5 2 1 4 2 *